Fake Dating my Baby Daddy

A Surprise Pregnancy, Friends to Lovers Romance

Josie Hart

Contents

1

Paige

"Oh my God!" Ava cried out, pushing through the crowds in the terminal to wrap her arms around me. "I can't believe you're finally here!" She looked at me with sparkling eyes as she held me at arm's length.

"It's been way too long," I said and hugged her again. "I'm still mad at you for moving, by the way."

Ava laughed and shook her head, her shoulder-length dark hair swaying. "Yeah, you keep telling me that."

Noah appeared with Warner on his hip.

"Hey, Paige," he said and hugged me with his free arm. I pinched Warner's cheeks.

"Look how big you're getting! What are they feeding you?"

Warner giggled and kicked his legs so that Noah would put him down, but Noah held tight.

"Don't put him down," Ava said gravely.

"I got him," Noah agreed and offered to take my rolling suitcase with his free hand.

"Seriously," Ava said, shaking her head. "He's at that age where he just runs, and he's so small and so quick, there's no way I can follow through the crowds."

I laughed. "He's adorable."

We walked through LAX to the parking area, where Ava took Warner to strap him into his car seat while Noah wrestled my bags into the car.

It had been six months since Noah and Ava had moved to LA. They'd decided to break away from Solomon, Forger, and Riggs, and Noah had come here to open his own law firm instead. The Cavaliers' legacy and the pressure on the families to conform and follow in their fathers' footsteps wasn't something they wanted Warner to suffer under.

"Do you miss home?" I asked Ava when we got into the sleek black car Noah drove.

"I don't miss Seattle," Ava admitted. "The weather here is incredible, we barely have any rain. Can you believe it?"

I giggled and shook my head. In Seattle, rain was a given.

"I miss the convenience of knowing where everything is, though. I'm getting better now, knowing where a couple of things are, but it's going to take time to really settle. Of course, I miss the people too."

I nodded. Video calls and the internet made the world a very small place, but being able to contact each other all the time was a poor substitute for seeing each other in person, and I'd missed my best friend so much.

"You made friends here, though, right?"

"Oh, yeah," Ava said, and Noah nodded, too. "It always helps to have some connections. Barney, the guy who helped Noah with a couple of litigations, introduced him to Parker Conrad."

"Oh my God, really?"

"Yeah, didn't I tell you that?"

"I'm sure I would have remembered."

"Yeah, I think I forgot to add that. Sorry."

This was exactly why our long-distance friendship drove me crazy. We talked all the time, but some of the big stuff fell through the cracks, and I was crazy curious.

"I feel like I'm missing out on all the good stuff!" I said tucking a strand of my light-brown hair behind one ear. "I wish I could be a part of it all."

Ava shot me an apologetic look, but I couldn't hold it against her. Since they'd moved to LA, it had been stressful to get everything going again. There was big demand on Noah to make his mark as a new lawyer in town, but being away from all the pressure at home was doing them both good. I could see how much happier they were, despite the stress they were under.

"There's a huge amount of gossip I *can* tell you," Ava said and twisted in her seat to look at me where I was sitting next to Warner's car seat. "Seriously, you'll die when you find out."

I laughed. "Okay, shoot."

"So, one of Parker Conrad's friends is Gavin Austin."

She offered me a pointed look.

"Who?" I asked.

Ava's jaw dropped. "Do you follow celebrity news at *all*?"

I burst out laughing. "You know me, Ava. I don't waste my time with stuff like that."

Ava groaned. "Yeah, yeah, okay. So, Gavin Austin is this hotshot in the business world, built his company from scratch, made a name for himself, all that. He's also drop-dead *gorgeous*."

Noah glanced at Ava. She put her hand on his leg and smiled sweetly at him.

"Never hotter than you, babe."

Noah grinned, and I laughed again. Ava and Noah were so good together.

"Anyway, he's been dating Tara Logan for the past three years."

She looked at me expectantly again. I shook my head slowly, and Ava sighed heavily.

"Yeah, I hoped you'd know that one, at least. She's the one who's been on all those dating shows, the reality star."

"Oh, I think I've heard the name."

"Right. So, she's really popular, and everyone thinks she's so great, but behind closed doors, she's a total..." Ava glanced at Warner before she mouthed the word *bitch* to me so that she kept it PG.

I giggled. "Really? Are those Gavin's words, or..."

"No, personal experience," Ava said.

"She's sort of right," Noah chimed in.

I rounded my mouth in an O of surprise. If Noah was weighing in on her level of bitch, it had to be serious. Noah was the least dramatic man I'd ever met—he didn't only avoid it, he ran in the opposite direction.

"They broke up recently," Ava said. "She's acting like the victim, but she's making Gavin's life hell. She has a healthy dose of venom in her.

"Oh, wow," I said. "You're in the know now that you're living in LA, huh?"

"Yeah." Ava shrugged nonchalantly, but she was enjoying being able to tell me all the gossip, not only from tabloids but firsthand.

"These reality TV stars are all the same," she continued. "We had the misfortune of spending time with her and her friends once when Gavin brought them along to a party. She wanted all the attention on her, cried when she couldn't get her way, then felt 'sick' and made Gavin take her home." She made finger quotes around the word.

"Honestly, I was glad when they left," Noah said, offering his opinion.

Ava put her hand on her husband's shoulder, and her fingers automatically dug into the muscle, looking for stress knots.

"I don't know if Parker said something, but he never brought her along again. The guys spent time together separately after that."

"I wouldn't take her anywhere if she acted like that, either," Noah scoffed.

"That sounds terrible," I said. I couldn't imagine a relationship where someone had to hide their SO because they couldn't behave themselves. "What's Gavin like? Is he an ass?"

"Oh, he's great," Ava said. "Tara makes him sound like the devil himself, but she's a woman scorned. He's very closed off but handsome as hell, and when he isn't playing his cards so close to his chest, he's really a wonderful person. He'll find someone soon enough. Wait, I'll show you."

She picked up her phone and opened a new browser tab. With a few swipes and taps, she brought up an image and handed the phone to me.

I stared at the photo of a man who was looking a bit drunk, leaning against the door of a pub. Despite that, he was handsome as hell. Ava had been right. Messy hair, dark eyes, a square jaw that would make any woman drool.

"I can see why she's unhappy about losing him."

Ava smirked at me. "Yeah?"

I nodded.

"You might meet him. Now that he's single, he might hang out with Parker a lot more, come to our events again... You never know what might happen, eh?" She winked at me.

I rolled my green eyes. "I'm not having some stupid summer fling in LA before I leave again," I said. "I'm not here for long enough."

Noah looked at me in the rearview mirror. "Good call. You just keep things on the straight and narrow. No need to flip over some guy who's supposed to be so *drop-dead gorgeous*."

Ava laughed and stroked her fingers through Noah's blond hair. "You know you're my everything. You're number one. The rest of the world comes in at a far second and counting down from there."

Noah smiled, satisfied, and Ava leaned over and kissed him on his cheek.

We arrived at Ava and Noah's home.

"I want a tour!" I said, looking up at the Tuscan-style mansion that stretched across a large plot of land with immaculate rolling lawns, an orchard, and an infinity pool that overlooked the suburban valley below them. "This place is incredible."

"You guys go," Noah said with a grin. "I've got the rest."

"Are you sure?" Ava asked.

Noah nodded with a smile. "You should catch up. Warner and I've got this. Right, big guy?"

Warner nodded enthusiastically and ran to the back of the car to try to open the trunk. Noah laughed and opened the trunk.

"I think you should carry this one for us," Noah said, giving Warner my travel pillow.

Ava grinned and planted a quick kiss on Noah's lips. "You're a saint."

"I know," he said with a wink.

Ava giggled, and her cheeks turned pink. They'd been married for a couple of years now, but they still looked like they were crazy in love like newlyweds.

"You guys are so good together," I said when Ava led me into the large house.

"When you have a great husband, it's so easy," Ava said.

I smiled, and she showed me the large entertainment rooms, the bar area, the patio, and the large pool. The house had eight en suite bedrooms and a large kitchen with state-of-the-art appliances that was to die for. My favorite part about the house was no matter which room we were in, the windows looked out over incredible gardens.

"This place is phenomenal," I said when Ava finished the tour. "What are you planning on doing with so many rooms? It's just the three of you. You'll have to have a ton of kids to fill them up."

Ava offered a small smile. "We're working on that."

"Yeah?" I asked. "Are you trying again?"

"Well..." Ava glanced at me. "I'm not supposed to say anything yet, we're announcing it in a couple of weeks, but I'm pregnant."

"What!" I cried out. "You didn't tell me!"

"I only found out about a week ago, and Noah and I decided to just ride it out for now. The first trimester can be so tricky, you know?"

I grabbed Ava into a hug. "I'm *so* happy for you, you have no idea! Your life is a fairy tale."

Ava laughed when I let go of her. "I'm not even going to argue with you. It's still early days, obviously, so we're just taking it as it comes now, but I'm really excited to have another baby."

I sighed. Ava deserved all the goodness in life. When she'd met Noah, she'd had it tough. Her dad had left them with a lot of debt when he passed away, and it had been hard on Ava and her mom. Noah had been her hero, and now that everything was taken care of, I wanted only good things for my friend.

My heart sank when I thought about Ava's life and how well things were going for her.

Ava picked up on my mood shift right away.

"Are you okay?"

"Yeah."

"You don't look okay."

I hesitated. "I don't really have a good reason not to be okay. I just feel... stuck."

Ava tilted her head. "Let's go to the kitchen. I'll make us coffee and get started on lunch, and you can tell me what's bothering you."

I nodded and followed Ava to the kitchen. When I offered to help, Ava ordered me to sit down at the breakfast nook.

"You're the pregnant one," I pointed out.

"You're the guest," Ava argued. "Let me be the queen of my castle and treat you."

I laughed and agreed and sat down in the booth at the large bay windows that looked out over a courtyard with wooden benches, terracotta tiles, and a fountain that babbled happily.

I watched as she prepared cups of coffee with the Nespresso machine.

"Tell me what's bugging you," Ava said.

I shook my head. "That's the thing. I don't know. Everything is perfect. I have a good job, I have a loving family, I have a future at the company... there's no reason for me to feel the way I do."

I'd worked as a PA at a company for a long time, but about two years ago, my boss had given me more responsibilities to see how I would manage, and when I'd done it well, he'd pushed me into a new role. I managed a whole department now because he'd said my skills and talents were going to waste as a mere personal assistant.

"How is your family?" Ava asked.

"Fine, all working and getting married and having babies… Mom and Dad are planning their thirtieth wedding anniversary, and they're more in love than ever." I had two sisters and two brothers. I was the middle child of five, and we were all pretty close. I was the only one still unmarried. At twenty-eight, my mom thought I was an old maid. My youngest sister was twenty-three and already married and pregnant.

"Your family is crazy," Ava said. "They're my inspiration, you know?"

"Really?"

"Yeah. I saw what it was like for you growing up with so many siblings, and I want that for my kids."

Ava was an only child. We'd been friends since middle school, and she used to spend a lot of weekends at my place, hanging out with my brothers and sisters. She'd always said she was jealous of me having such a big family. I'd always told her I was jealous of the peace and quiet she had.

"That's nice to know," I said with a smile, but my smile faded quickly. "Do you see why I have no reason to feel so stuck?"

"You haven't found anyone new?" Ava asked.

I shook my head. "After Scott, I haven't really looked. I think there's something wrong with me."

"Why?" Ava brought a steaming cup of coffee to me and returned to make herself a cup of decaf coffee.

"Because Scott wanted to give me the world. A stable home, kids, everything any woman wants. I dumped him."

Ava glanced sidelong at me. "Just because that's supposed to be the ideal doesn't mean that it's *your* ideal. What do you really want?"

"I don't know. I think that's half the problem," I said. "I'm just so tired of everything being so perfectly bland. I want something different, something challenging, something unexpected. You know? I want…" I laughed, shaking my head. "I don't know what I want, and it's driving me crazy. Mom keeps saying I should go to London, but I don't know if that will solve my problems."

"Oh, right, with your dad's European passport?"

"Right. I just don't see how if I can't find happiness here, I'll be able to find happiness there. Isn't that something that should come from within?"

"Very wise," Ava said with a smile.

"I'll miss you too much, anyway. I can already not stand the short distance between LA and Seattle."

"Hmm," Ava said, taking ingredients for sandwiches out of the fridge. "I think this break will give you the answers you need."

"Yeah?"

"Of course, it worked wonders for us."

It wasn't quite the same thing, but I didn't say that.

"And I love seeing you again," Ava said with a smile.

I nodded. I loved seeing her, too. I'd missed her so much. Life in Seattle just hadn't been the same since she'd left.

The topic switched to other, lighter things. Ava told me about her part-time work as a lawyer. Since she'd had Warner, she'd scaled down to only work half-days so that she could be with him, and here in LA, she'd gotten an opportunity to work on an hourly basis as and when it worked for her. It was the perfect arrangement, especially for a mother who was going to have another baby.

Noah and Warner joined us not too long after, and we decided it was a perfect day to enjoy the weather.

We spent the day at the beach and went out for dinner in the evening—Noah insisted we were going to celebrate my being in LA the right way. I loved how positive he was about my friendship with Ava.

Some guys were clingy and possessive, jealous if their other halves had a good relationship with someone, but Noah encouraged girl talk and did what he could to keep Warner busy so we could chat and catch up.

He was the kind of husband everyone wished they could have—Prince Charming personified. I wished more of those existed, but I'd looked, and they just... didn't.

I had to settle for being alone, I guess.

By the time I was in bed, it was almost midnight, and my head spun from too much wine at the restaurant. I loved the way the room slowly turned around me, and I felt lighter than air.

All I needed now was a good fuck. Wine made me so horny, and it had been a while since I'd been with someone.

I curled on the bed and closed my eyes, slowly sliding my hands down my body. My nerve endings were on fire, and my body craved to be touched. It sucked that I was on my own, but I didn't have anything better right now. I had a good imagination—I could make this work.

Gavin Austin flashed before me, and I stilled. Why was I thinking about him? Probably because he was fucking hot, and if there were *someone* I would have liked to kiss right now, to lick, to suck, to taste, to fuck... it would be him.

I ran my hands over my breasts, arching my back, and imagined it was him. I pictured unbuttoning his shirt and pushing it over his shoulders. He did the same to me, pulling my top over my head, and I took a moment to admire a spectacular chest. A face like his would have an incredible body beneath it, I just knew it.

Lust gripped me, and I shivered when his hands rested on my breasts. His touch was gentle, teasing. He massaged me, kneading my breasts until I gasped and moaned. I pinched my nipples, making them hard and imagined it was him, rolling them between his fingers while his face was at my neck, nibbling the soft skin.

I imagined him lowering his head, working his way onto my chest. He dipped his head and kissed a trail of fire across the swells of my breasts, and I got wetter. He grinded himself against me, his cock thick and hard, and when he sucked a nipple into his mouth, I slid one hand between my legs.

I gasped softly, keeping it down. I was a houseguest. My fingers found my clit, and I slowly drew circles around it, working myself up. I thought about Gavin's eyes, deep and dark and broody in that photo. His breathing got deeper in my mind's eye as he worshipped my breasts, sucking and licking one nipple before he moved to the other.

I was getting closer and fast. I switched from imagining Gavin paying attention to my nipples to us being naked on the bed, with him on top of me. His tongue was in my mouth, my hands in his messy hair, and he tasted like a walking orgasm. I gasped when he positioned himself between my legs, and his cock pushed against my entrance. I moaned when he pushed into me. Heat washed through me as I rubbed myself faster and faster, picturing Gavin bucking his hips. His cock had to be delicious, sliding in and out of me.

I moaned, struggling to keep it down, and turned my head into the pillow to muffle my sounds. I bucked my hips against my own hand and ached for a cock to fill me up. I wanted Gavin to slide into me, to fuck me harder and harder. I crept closer and closer to the edge. At first, I wanted him on top of me, riding me until I orgasmed. Then I wanted him to flip me over. I pictured him dragging a finger slowly down my spine before his cock found my entrance again, and he slid into me in one push. With one hand cupping my breast and the other on my hip, he fucked me until I cried out his name again and again.

The orgasm rocked through my body, spreading from my core, and I moaned into the pillows, letting the pleasure take me away. It was sharp and intense and over quickly.

I lay on the bed, gasping, trying to catch my breath again. The image of Gavin, naked, slowly faded.

I tugged the sheets up to my chin and rolled onto my side.

I needed to get laid, I decided. Even if it meant nothing, just to get it out of my system. Of course, I doubted I would find someone as delicious as Gavin, but a girl could dream. I let out a sigh, and between the rush of satisfaction from the orgasm and the wine still in my system, sleep dragged me under.

Just before I slipped away, I flashed on Gavin's face again. Not naked and filled with lust as he'd been in my fantasy just now, but guarded as he'd been in that photo. Those eyes... what was it about his eyes? I didn't have time to pull it apart before I fell asleep.

"Welcome to *Metropolitan Prime*, where you'll find the latest celebrity news—and gossip—as it happens! I'm your host, Kieran Cohen, and joining me tonight is none other than Tara Logan!"

The audience erupted in cheers.

The camera panned out to show Tara Logan, with a beautiful smile, glittering in a gold sequined dress. Kieran Cohen sat down next to her.

"We all know you from shows like Love Lost and Found, Forever Feuds, Love is Real, and Love, Love, Love, and tonight, this lady of love is right here with us."

"It's such a pleasure to be here with you," Tara said with a bright smile.

"With me?" Kieran said, feigning surprise.

"Of course. With the experience, it's safe to say I know men, and you're one of the good ones." She nudged Kieran, and he faked a blush.

"Compliments like that will go straight to my head if you're not careful," Kieran said.

"Which head?" Tara asked sweetly.

"Oh, oh"—Kieran laughed—"I see what you did there. That's why you're America's favorite. You're all things nice… with a dash of spice!" He winked at the audience.

"Now, all jokes aside, things haven't been so easy on you lately, huh?"

Tara pursed her lips, and her large eyes widened a little more.

"We all heard about your recent split from business mogul Gavin Austin. You were together for quite some time."

"Three years," Tara said, nodding. "We were supposed to celebrate our third anniversary next week, actually."

The audience awwed in sympathy, and Tara offered them a watery smile, her eyes shimmering with tears.

"That must be hard."

"It is," Tara said. "It's been a lot harder than I've let on. With Gavin, it was nothing like the game shows, you know? I mean, we all want to find love, and we all strive to find the perfect match, but Gavin... he was that guy I didn't see coming, and he swept me off my feet. He made me feel like a princess"—she glanced at the audience—"until he didn't."

"Was there trouble in paradise?"

"What relationship doesn't have its ups and downs, right?" Tara asked. She swallowed hard as if trying to stop her tears. "I thought he was my forever. I was ready to spend the rest of my life with him. I gave him everything... clearly, he didn't feel the same."

"Did you know?" Kieran asked gently.

Tara shook her head, and a tear rolled over her cheek. "I thought we were going to be one of those rare couples that makes it through. I didn't see it coming at all. One day, he told me he loved me, and the next." Her face crumpled, and Kieran Cohen waved the camera away from her.

"I'm sorry, folks, that's all for now. It's a touchy subject, but we'll keep an eye on Tara and make sure she's okay, so not to worry! Before we know it, the star will be back on her feet and stealing hearts! Thank you for joining us on *Metropolitan Prime*, where we keep it real!"

2

Gavin

"To freedom!" I cried out, lifting my tequila shooter into the air.

Ryan and Parker lifted their shot glasses, and we clinked them together before throwing them back.

"It's about fucking time, man," Parker said.

"Yeah, I know," I said grimly. "I waited too long." I waved at the bartender to bring me a refill on my whiskey. Why didn't the asshole just leave the bottle? He knew we would finish the damn thing. We were good for it.

"For us, too," Parker said when the bartender nodded at me.

I'd just dumped Tara, the woman I'd been dating for the past three years, and it was a weight off my shoulders to be rid of her.

"Do you think this is going to be a clean cut?" Ryan asked.

I snorted. "Hell, no. She'll already be out there, crying on the shoulders of every evening show host where she can get a spot, making them love her and hate me. Tara knows exactly how to make someone's life a living hell. She's fine-tuned it, turned it into an art. She's a specialist. No, a *prodigy*."

Ryan and Parker burst out laughing. Ryan pushed a hand into his auburn hair, leaning on the bar.

"If she's that bad—"

"She's worse," I chipped in. "She was more upset about me taking my credit card back than us breaking up. I think that was the part where she actually started crying."

"—then why did you date her for so long?"

I shrugged. The room spun sufficiently around me, and where blood should have filled my veins, I was pretty sure I was made of alcohol now. Alcohol and relief.

"You know how it goes... you hold out hope that shit's going to change. I mean, she was really nice when we first met. Sexy, funny, pretty, she was the whole package."

"Until she wasn't," Ryan said. "And no, I don't know how it goes."

Parker and I both blinked at Ryan.

"I don't hold on to women long enough to be disappointed by what they aren't." Ryan shrugged nonchalantly.

Parker and I looked at each other before we burst out laughing again.

"You're full of shit," I said. "I know you like Sam."

"Yeah, she's nice, but I don't know how long it will last," Ryan said. "I think you did the right thing."

"Great to have you on board," I said, and when the whiskey glasses arrived, I lifted mine in salute to Ryan. I turned to Parker. "And you... you're fucking lucky you ended up with a woman who's worth your while. Seriously, Em is an angel. We all love her."

Parker grinned. "Thanks. I'm pretty fond of her, too."

"Jackass," Ryan said, laughing.

Emily and Ryan were twins, and Ryan and Parker had been friends for a long time. I'd only met them at Ryan's gym a short while ago, but there had been a lot of shit between them at one stage. The story went that Ryan had been pissed when he'd found out Emily and Parker had gotten together, and just when they'd thought all was lost, she'd wound up pregnant with Parker's baby.

Now, they were happily married, with a five-year-old boy and a three-year-old girl, and Parker was one of the few guys who'd really hit it big in life when it came to love and family.

"You'll find your happily ever after," Parker said. "You just keep looking."

I snorted and sipped my whiskey.

"Not all of us are gifted with your good looks, your fortune, and someone as gracious as your wife."

"What the fuck are you talking about?" Parker laughed. "You have the broody tall-dark-and-handsome thing going, you have a metric fuck ton of money, all you need is the woman."

"Hey, two out of three is still a pass," I said. "I'll take it."

"You just focus on getting through this shit with Tara, and then you're home free and good to go another round," Ryan said. "In the meantime, you're going to want to do three things." He counted them off on his fingers. "Drink as much as you want, fuck as many women as you want, and come to my gym as much as you can."

"What's the gym part for?"

"It's good business if I promote my gym," Ryan said with a shrug.

We burst out laughing.

"My PR manager is going to have a field day if I spend all day and night drinking and fucking," I said. "She's already unhappy about the ripples this split is going to cause. Tara can't keep her dirty laundry off the internet, so of course, all the social media channels are full of it, and it's making me look bad. She's the poor little princess who got hurt, and I'm the evil asshole who kicked her out." I shook my head. If the world had any idea how many faces she wore... I had a rule about people with faces. My limit was down to one. One face, one personality, thank you very much. It had taken me too long to figure out that to Tara, it was all a game.

"It will blow over," Parker said. "Trust me, some other scandal will happen, and then your story will be forgotten."

"That's what I get for dating an influencer," I said, shaking my head. "I should have known getting involved with her was trouble."

"Love is blind, my friend," Ryan said. "I would have made the same mistake."

I nodded. I'd met Tara backstage after I'd done an interview on *Money Talk Weekly*, and she'd been there to collect a check for the reality TV show she'd done at the time. One thing had led to another, and she'd blown me away. She really had been the whole package, and I'd believed she wanted me so much. She'd seemed like the kind of woman I could do forever with. Until I realized it was my money she was after.

Influencers like Tara didn't make their own money, every image was curated to make it look like she lived the high life, but the truth was she hadn't had a lot when I met her.

Now, after I'd dumped her, she was back to square one, and, boy, was she pissed.

"I hope someone's scandal happens fast," I said. "I don't know how much more I can take of the paps following me around. It's like the tabloids have nothing better to do than send photographers to harass people."

"One man's pain is another man's pleasure," Parker said.

"I hope she finds someone else soon, so they can latch their attention onto them and leave me alone. God, for three years I've felt like a celebrity just because they've been running around after her."

Parker and Ryan nodded sympathetically while I ranted about my ex. They were great friends, coming with me to drown my sorrows, to celebrate my newfound freedom, and to listen to me go on and on about her until it was out of my system.

By tomorrow, I would feel better, and my life could keep going.

"What about you?" I asked Parker. "Are you and Em going to have more kids?"

"I don't know," Parker said. "We haven't talked about it. It's a nice even number now, you know?"

I nodded. "Yeah, it sounds right. It's weird that all of our friends are married and having kids now when I'm back to being single."

"I'm not," Ryan said. "I'll be single with you."

I laughed. "Don't just get rid of Samantha, she's actually a good one."

"Yeah, yeah."

"Do you want kids?" Parker asked.

I shrugged. "I don't know. I thought I did when Tara was going on and on about it, but a lot of what I wanted then was really what *she* wanted. Having kids is a big sacrifice, and I don't know if I'm ready for something like that."

"When you find the right person, everything changes," Parker said. "Marriage, kids… it all seems so natural. I couldn't imagine being with someone before I met Emily, and now, I can't imagine my life without her."

I was happy for Parker. Really. He worked hard, he'd been through hell and back in his life, and he deserved for things to come easy now.

My life just wasn't like his. He kept talking about finding the right woman, but I wasn't so sure that was reserved for all of us.

When I looked at how things had been with my parents, there wasn't exactly proof of it, either. I hadn't grown up in a family where my mom and dad had been happily married, and it was this great example of what I could aim for one day.

My dad had been a raging alcoholic. He hadn't been abusive—I guess we were lucky—but he hadn't given a shit about our needs either. He'd spent all his money on alcohol, he'd pissed away anything that mattered, and when my mom left him, it had taken him three weeks to realize she was gone.

I'd been a teenager and doing my own thing by then, but that shit stays with a kid and "happily ever after" was something that happened in movies, not in real life. Except maybe Parker's.

"Last round," the bartender called.

I frowned and looked at the time.

"Shit, is it four already?" We'd drank the whole fucking night away. "I better get going. Isn't Em going to be pissed at you?"

Parker shook his head. "She knows you need me. She's cool about stuff like that."

I shook my head. "She's really one in a million."

"Yeah," Parker said with a grin. "But just now, when the sun comes up, and I'm hungover as shit and groggy with so little sleep, I'm going to have two kids jumping on the bed asking for pancakes. I'll pay my dues, don't you worry."

I laughed, and we paid our bill before we got up and left the bar.

I stumbled when I stepped outside, and camera flashes went off everywhere. I squinted against the bright lights and lifted my arms to cover my face.

Fuck, why were they still here?

"Get lost!" I called out, trying to flag a cab. I hadn't driven here because I'd known I was going to get hammered. Now, I regretted not figuring something else out.

"Come on," Parker said, putting his arm around my shoulders. "I have the car here, I'll get the driver to drop you."

"Me too," Ryan said and caught up to us in a jog.

We climbed into the back of Parker's car, and the driver pulled into the road. I'd never been so grateful for tinted windows.

"Thanks, man," I said when the car slid through the streets of LA. "You're going to be on the news too, now."

"It will be fine," Parker said.

I nodded. I wasn't so sure that was true. At least not for me, not for a while. The pictures of me stumbling out of the pub drunk out of my brackets would be all over the internet tomorrow, and Melissa was going to have a field day trying to get it all under control. My poor PR manager didn't get paid nearly enough for all the shit she'd had to put up with since Tara had been in my life.

Another reason I should have gotten rid of Tara sooner. But everything always looked so much better in hindsight. In the moment, I hadn't known what would come. I hadn't known how she would fuck shit up for me.

Well, rather late than never. She was out of my life now, and soon, the next scandal would come, and they would hopefully forget all about me.

That was all I wanted. I'd never wanted to be in the limelight. When I'd started my company, all I'd wanted to do was create a life that wasn't as hard as it had been when I'd been a kid. I'd resolved to make enough money that I would never have to go to bed hungry. The fame had come with Tara, and I was glad to be rid of it.

I just wanted this whole shitshow to be over.

3

Paige

When I woke up, I rolled onto my back in the king-sized four-poster bed and stretched lazily under the sheets. Ava and Noah's house was like a palace, and staying here was staying in the lap of luxury. Forget five-star accommodation, this was incredible.

My door slowly opened, and I frowned.

Warner's little face peeked around the door. He had his dad's blond hair and his mom's dark eyes.

"Hey, buddy," I said with a smile and sat up.

Warner grinned at me and ran into the room when I acknowledged him. He clambered onto the bed and dove onto my pillows. "What are you doing here?"

"Mommy's sleeping," Warner said. "Can we watch TV?"

"I guess we can," I said and looked around for the remote to the TV in my bedroom. All the guest bedrooms had televisions, couches by large windows, and bathrooms the size of my living room back home.

"What are we watching?" I asked.

"Fawpaws!" Warner cried out.

"What?"

I flipped through the channels, trying to figure out what he was saying to me.

"What's Fawpaws?"

When I flipped past a cartoon channel, Warner cheered.

"Oh, *Fire Pals*," I said, reading the show title and giggling. "Right."

"Fawpaws are so cool," Warner said and bounced on the bed as dogs and cats all raced out of a fire station on a big fire truck. The show was very basic, but I loved Warner's reaction as his eyes were glued to the screen.

We'd watched about fifteen minutes of the show when someone knocked on my door.

"Yes?"

Ava popped her head in.

"Oh, there you are! Warner, you little monkey!"

Warner put his hands to his mouth and giggled.

"He got away from Noah just now when he fell asleep on the couch. I'm so sorry."

"Don't be." I laughed. "We've been watching *Fawpaws*." I patted the bed and scooched over to give Ava a space, too. She climbed onto the bed and made herself comfortable. Warner climbed into her lap and promptly sucked his thumb.

"He's adorable," I said with a smile.

"Yeah, I keep wondering how I'm going to fit two in my lap, but we'll figure it out." She ran her fingers through Warner's blond hair.

We watched the show together for a while until Noah stumbled into the room, bleary-eyed, his hair sticking up at all angles.

"There you are," Noah said. "I'm so sorry, babe."

"Daddy, your hair!" Warner cried out and laughed, kicking his feet.

Noah finger-combed his hair. "It's bedhead," he said with a grin. "Or *couchhead*, as it were." He walked to the bed and grabbed Warner, tickling him until Warner squealed with laughter. "We're supposed to bring the ladies breakfast in bed! Come on, let's go find something to toast."

Warner jumped up with a cheer, and they left the room. Noah waved at us over his shoulder and blew Ava a kiss before he disappeared.

The *Fire Pals* jingle started as the credits rolled.

"I'm so sick of this show," Ava said. "We watch it day and night. Warner can't get enough of it."

I picked up the remote. "I'll change it to something else."

Ava shook her head. "No, let's get ready and go to the store. I want to grab a couple of things for that barbecue we're having soon, and we're dangerously low on my gluten-free crackers. I'll indulge in the other stuff if I don't get more, and it will go straight to my hips."

I laughed. "You look great."

Ava walked out of the room to get ready, and I had a quick shower.

Ava wrangled Warner into his car seat and handed him a snack. Going on outings kept him busy, too.

"Okay, so tell me about this barbecue," I said. "I feel like I'm being thrown in the deep end. I won't know anyone."

"You'll know me," Ava said and squeezed my hand. "The others are great, too. Parker is married to a gem of a woman named Emily. She drew me into a few social circles, and we grab coffee a few times a week and get the kids together."

"It's great you have some new friends," I said. A pang of... *something* shot into my chest. I tried to dissect it. It wasn't jealousy—I wanted Ava to be happy, and I would never want her to be without friends in a new place. I just hated that I wasn't here to see how her life was changing and getting better.

I also hated that my life was so stagnant and *boring*. I didn't have anything exciting in my life, like moving to new places, making new friends, or having new experiences.

"Parker is the middle of three brothers, and Sebastian, we call him Bas, and Chaz are both married, too. You'll love them—they're so down to earth, and the women are like sisters now. They go out of their way to draw everyone in. I felt so welcome when I first met them, and I'm sure it will be the same for you."

"It's so great you landed on your feet down here," I said. "Your new friends sound amazing... I would have been jealous if I wasn't so crazy happy your life is what it's supposed to be now."

Ava smiled at me. She'd had a very tough run with her dad dumping her into a lot of debt and her mother going into depression. Her young adult life had started out with financial stress that shouldn't have been hers, and she'd had to carry the weight of the world. Now, with all these great-sounding people in her life, she could be carefree. Even with being married with one child and another on the way.

Happiness came in all shapes and sizes.

I just wished mine would present itself, too. No matter what it looked like.

We stopped, and I helped Ava set up the stroller so we could put Warner in before we walked to the mall.

I was excited about the barbecue, meeting the people who were part of Ava's life now, and maybe making a friend or two for myself.

Not that I expected the friendships would be long-lasting—I was going back to Seattle soon—but I was excited about the opportunity to shake things up. Maybe it wasn't the adventure I hoped I would have one day, but it was a start. Who knew, maybe something bigger could come of it.

A girl could only hope.

4

Gavin

Whe I walked into the office, Melissa Stone's face was pinched, her blue eyes serious.

"I know, I know." I sighed.

"I don't think you do," Melissa said. "We talked about this."

My head throbbed like a bitch, and I was sick to my stomach. Drinking as much as I had didn't feel so great today.

"No, Mel, *you* talked about this," I said. "I did you a favor by letting you know beforehand I was breaking up with her. The rest is not my fault. What did you think I was going to do, sit at home and pout?"

"I was hoping that was what you would do."

"Pouting doesn't look good on me." I dropped into my leather chair and opened my laptop.

"I think most people will disagree," Melissa said with a grin. "But it's the staying-at-home part I hoped you would listen to. We both knew she was going to throw a temper tantrum and it would be all over the news. Tara Logan doesn't know how to do anything quietly.

She needs the rest of the world to know of her every move or it doesn't count in her book, and right now, *you're* a part of her every move."

I groaned. "It will blow over. It's not a big deal."

Melissa pursed her lips. "It's bigger than you think. Have you seen the tabloids? The photos? Have you heard what she's saying?"

I shook my head. I'd carefully avoided anything to do with her. It had been hard work, but I was happy to say that I hadn't read a single article or seen a single TV broadcast with her in it. "I choose not to indulge her."

Melissa only raised her eyebrows at me.

"What?"

"Here." She pushed a tablet across the desk, open on a tabloid article. I started reading, and the further I went, the more my gut sank to my shoes.

"What the *fuck*!"

"Yeah, I know."

"You know it's a load of shit, right? If I was drinking, it was with her, and we were both equally drunk! You know I'm not like this."

The article laid out in no uncertain terms how Tara had been taken advantage of in our relationship, how she'd put on a happy face for the public, but behind closed doors, she had to deal with my rampant drinking.

"I know that's not how it is, but she knows it's a weakness."

I all but threw the tablet down. Gone were the days when things were printed on hard-copy newspaper, and I could slam it down on the desk or rip the articles to shreds. It had been a lot more satisfying.

"How am I still stuck in his shadow more than a decade down the line?" I asked. "I thought after I broke away from my family, I would leave him in the past, but I'm haunted by his shitty choices every fucking day." I ran my hands down my face.

They'd drawn a direct line between the bullshit Tara spewed about my drinking and the reality of who my dad was.

"It's resurfacing now because Tara knows it's a touchy subject," Melissa said gently. "She's using it to her advantage. If it wasn't that, she would have said it was something else—whatever else might have been an issue in your life. That's why I need you to watch yourself."

I shook my head and regretted it. "I know you're looking out for me, and you're doing your job, but I'm over trying to please everyone. It's been three years of putting on a face, and I'm done." I pressed my fingers against my temples, trying to alleviate the headache, then I opened my desk drawers, looking for Advil. I had to have some here somewhere.

My phone buzzed on my desk. I'd put it on vibrate. When I glanced at the number, I scowled. It was my dad.

I silenced the call and cursed under my breath, searching for the damn Advil. When I came up empty-handed, Melissa was watching me.

She hesitated.

"What?" Had she seen my dad's call? If she lectured me on that now...

Maybe another drink would help. Bite the dog that bit you, right?

"The thing is," she said carefully, "you knew you were going to be in the spotlight when you started dating her. I warned you."

"Yeah, yeah." I groaned. "I played the game, Mel. I followed the stupid rules, and I did as I was told. Now, I'm done with her, and I'm sick of the charade."

Melissa shook her head. "It's going to take a while longer to pick up the pieces. Here is where the real work starts."

I stood and walked to the full-length windows that looked out over downtown LA.

"Hungover?" she asked.

"I feel like death warmed up."

"I never understand that saying."

"Yeah... me either, actually. I'm pretty sure it means it's really bad. My hangover is really bad."

I looked out over the city, and we were together in silence for a while.

"Don't tell me it's not over," I said softly.

Melissa sighed. "I'm sorry, Gavin. It's only just beginning. She's going to cause shit for as long as she can. Hell hath no fury like a woman scorned."

I pulled a face. I hated that saying, but it was true. And Tara was about as vehement as they got. When she was slighted, the whole world trembled. I'd felt her wrath before—being with her for three years hadn't been smooth sailing. I'd known all hell would break loose when I dumped her.

"I guess I just hoped she would be mature about this," I said to Melissa, looking over my shoulder at her.

"If she was mature, Gav, you wouldn't have dumped her."

That was the truth. If everything had been fine, Tara would still have been my girlfriend, and I wouldn't have to deal with this shit.

"What do you want me to do?"

"Stay out of the public eye for a while unless you're on your best behavior," Melissa said. "I know it's horrible to have to keep putting on an act and watching your every move now that it's over, but it will blow over eventually."

I sighed. "Yeah."

"You won't be stuck with this forever. She'll find someone new, and then the whole cycle will start over for her, and you'll be free."

I nodded. Melissa was right, as usual. It was why I'd hired her—almost seven years ago now. I'd looked for a PR manager to help me out with my business image after the first time someone had dug up some dirt on my family and it had come out that my dad was an alcoholic. Melissa had been with me since then, picking up the pieces when my life fell apart, helping me keep the company's name high so that my shares did well and business was good.

She wasn't only a PR manager anymore. She'd become a friend.

"Thank you, Mel. I'll try."

"Just keep to private events for now. I'll keep my finger on the pulse and let you know when the storm dies down."

I nodded, and Melissa slipped the tablet into her leather handbag before she stood.

"I'll be in touch," she said. "Just try to breathe through this, and remind yourself that in every breakup, there's a psycho ex."

"Yeah?" I asked with a grin.

"Yeah. If you've never had one... well, I have bad news for you."

I laughed. "Thanks for that."

She left me behind smiling, and when the office door closed, I turned back to my desk. My smile faded fast as I sat down behind my laptop.

Damn it, I'd hoped I could get out and live it up now that I was single. I wanted to party, dance and drink, and work my way through a bunch of rebound women so that I could feel better about it all.

Was I heartbroken? Not exactly.

I'd been the one to dump Tara, and I'd thought about it for a while. It didn't hurt me the way it did for her—it had been out of the blue when I'd called it off. She'd whined about money and choices, and I just hadn't been able to take it anymore—I'd wanted to wait longer, to find an opportune moment. There wasn't ever an opportune moment to break someone's heart, was there? I'd snapped and dumped her then and there.

That didn't mean that it didn't still smart.

It wasn't fun to find out that the woman I loved was only after me for my money. I should have known, but I'd wanted to see something different in her. I'd wanted her to be more.

My will was only enough to make so much happen. After a while, I couldn't look past the facts anymore.

My phone buzzed again, and I eyed it dubiously, but it was Parker's name on the caller ID this time.

"How's your head?" Parker asked.

"Bad enough that I had my phone on silent this whole time," I said with a chuckle. "Don't we ever learn?"

"No," Parker said. "The biggest lie we've ever told ourselves is 'I'm never drinking again.' "

I laughed. "Yeah, that sounds about right. I say it every time I drink, and in a couple of days, I'm *thirsty*."

We laughed together.

"So, I saw the tabloids," Parker said, his laughter fading away. "Em told me about the show, too…"

I cursed under my breath. "It's a fucking mess."

"What does Mel say?"

"She says I should hang low, stay out of the public unless I've got my shit straight, and wait for it to die down."

"Yeah, that makes sense. She won't go at it forever."

"God, I hope not," I groaned.

"So, now that you're all about staying out of the public eye, you know we're having that barbecue this weekend, right? Why don't you join us?"

Parker had mentioned the barbecue before, but I hadn't wanted to go. Tara hadn't been the kind of person I could take places. She'd made everything about her, and none of my friends deserved to have to entertain her. She'd slowly isolated me from my friends, cutting me off so she could have me all to herself.

Now that I was single, there was no reason to decline invitations.

"Okay," I said. "Why not, it could be fun."

"It will be a lot of fun. It won't be anything wild because the kids will be there. Chaz and Holly are bringing Sydney, too, and the twins, and Noah, Ava, and Warner are coming."

"A regular daycare center."

"Barbecue care," Parker joked. "It will be very PG."

"It sounds like exactly what I need."

"I think so, too."

I hesitated. "Did you read it?"

"Yeah."

"It's a bunch of crap."

"Yeah," Parker said again. "Have you talked to your mom?"

"No. I haven't told her yet, but she'll hear it somewhere, I'm sure. I'll call her later."

"And your dad?"

I stifled a groan. "The SOB tried to call now that he's in the news again, indirectly. I don't talk to him, you know that."

"I was just asking."

I clenched my jaw. The last time I talked to my dad was when I turned eighteen, and I hadn't legally needed anything from him anymore. To me, he'd died that day. He tried to call at regular intervals these days, but it was far too little, far too late. What the fuck was he trying to reach out to me for when he'd had my whole childhood to build a relationship? I didn't know where he was or what he did, and I didn't care.

"Don't give them ammo," Parker said.

"Who?"

"The public."

"What's that supposed to mean?" I challenged.

"I'm just saying that if something isn't a problem to you, they can't use it against you."

"I don't have a problem with my dad."

Parker was quiet long enough that I knew he didn't agree with me. I wasn't going to argue with him about it. He didn't *know*. We'd only been friends a couple of years. All he knew about my dad was what I'd told him and what had been in the news. Nothing more.

"I'll see you this weekend," I said, ending the call before I said something I shouldn't. Parker was a good friend, and I knew he meant well. He just didn't realize that his perfect life blinded him to how tough shit could get out here sometimes. He'd been through his fair share of pain, but every man's journey was unique, and I wanted him to butt out of mine.

"It will be good to see you, buddy."

"Text me whatever I'm supposed to bring along."

"I'll check with Em and let you know," Parker said before he ended the call.

A barbecue with a bunch of kids and family people didn't sound like my favorite pastime, but it was out of the public eye, which would make Melissa happy, and the kids weren't my responsibility, so I could drink, and that would make me happy. It would be good to hang out with friends again without having to worry about how something would come across and that Tara would embarrass herself or me somehow.

I turned my attention back to my laptop and focused on work. I'd started this company from scratch and built it into the leviathan it was today. It wasn't going to run itself.

At least, work was always a constant I could rely on. When everything else went to shit, there was still the company, and that helped.

Other people had a significant other who were there, no matter what. I had my business.

To each their own, right?

5

Paige

On the day of the barbecue, Noah and Ava packed a bunch of toys into the car for Warner to play with, Ava prepared a salad, and we drove to a house just a couple of blocks away from where Noah and Ava lived.

The large house was modern, with tropical-themed gardens and a beautiful water feature that wound all around the house. Koi fish, large and small, glittered under the gentle ripples of the water. A large Monstera with broad, glossy leaves was the statement piece by the front door.

Emily opened for us herself, and I was introduced to a woman with dark hair and an easy smile. I liked her right away, and I could see why Ava did too.

"It's so good to see you again!" Emily said to Ava, giving her a hug. "And you must be Paige. I hear so much about you, it's great to finally put a face to the name!"

She ushered us all inside, and Warner was immediately met by a little boy who looked almost exactly like Emily and a girl who could have been his twin. They were excited to see each other.

"This is Tommy and Maddi." Emily introduced them. "Take the toys to the playhouse, kids. Show Warner what Daddy built!" She giggled when they ran to the door that led to the back garden. "Parker built a playhouse for them. He'll tell you all about how he did it all himself, but he hired a contractor with a whole team. Don't tell him I said so, but his contribution was pointing his finger while he had a beer in his hand."

Noah laughed. "He makes big bucks, he should pay a specialist to do it."

"Oh, I agree," Emily said. "It's just the way he talks about it." Her eyes danced with laughter. "Men are like kids. They just want a gold star."

"Oh come on," Noah said.

"And you can get your gold star in a minute," Emily said with a wink.

A tall man with dark hair came in from outside.

"Hey, man," he said to Noah and clapped him on the back. "I thought I heard voices and figured Warner didn't walk himself over." He held out a hand to me. "I'm Parker."

"The handyman," I said with a smirk.

Parker looked like he wasn't sure if I was joking or not and glanced at Ava and Emily, who both erupted in laughter.

"I built the playhouse myself," Parker said. "I'm serious. A lot of workmanship went into that thing."

"And it's a thing of pride," Emily said, kissing her husband on the lips. "The kids love it. Come on, have a look, and we'll introduce you to the rest of them."

I swallowed hard. "The rest of them" sounded like a big party.

We walked through the house, and every room was incredible. It was like one of those glamorous homes out of a luxury home design magazine.

"Your home is absolutely beautiful, Emily."

"Oh, thanks. I'm still working on it, but between projects and the kids, I don't get much time to really make it spectacular."

I glanced at Ava and lowered my voice. "This isn't spectacular?" The place was a palace of luxury, every room designed with a beautiful theme, paintings with colors that popped, and furniture that looked like it came right out of a catalog.

"Emily's an interior designer," Ava explained. "She owns a very large, very successful company."

"Ah, that explains a lot."

We stepped onto the patio, and a group of men were huddled around a massive industrial-sized barbecue meant for entertaining, beers in hand. The women sat talking to each other on a set of sleek modern wicker couches nearby. The sun filtered through elegant white curtains that draped down from the pagoda, and everyone looked comfortable sipping cool drinks.

I glanced at the playhouse. It was a multilevel wooden structure complete with a ball pit, slide, and swing set. The centerpiece was a small house; through the doors and windows, I spotted miniature furniture. The kids were laughing and chasing each other around.

The men and women all came and greeted Noah and Ava like they were long-lost friends. It was so good to see Ava had settled in so well.

"Okay, introductions," Ava said. "Everyone, this is Paige."

"We've heard so much about you," a blonde woman said.

"Everyone keeps saying that," I said, my cheeks coloring.

"That's because I can't stop talking about you," Ava said with a grin. "Okay, that's Chaz and his wife, Holly. That graceful young woman over there"—she pointed at a teenager drawing at a table not too far off—"is their daughter Sydney."

Sydney looked up and hooked her hair behind her ear.

"I'm not a woman yet," she said and blushed. "I'm just thirteen."

She looked much older.

"Those two rug rats over there"—Ava pointed at identical girls with light hair and delicate features—"are Danica and Danielle, the twins."

"I don't think I'll remember any of the names," I said, feeling overwhelmed.

"That's okay! We don't expect you to right away, and we'll help you figure it out," Holly said with a smile.

"I'm Lexi," the blonde said. "That one's mine." She pointed at a man who looked a lot like Chaz and Parker. I knew they were brothers, but if I hadn't known it, I could have guessed right away. "Bas is the barbecue master."

Bas snorted. "No one else can do it right."

They all laughed.

"Ryan and Samantha and their friend Gavin are a little late," Parker said, looking at his watch with a frown. "But you've met the family. Make yourself at home, and if the kids want more cookies... don't let them convince you. They get a bunch of energy now, and then they crash. It's a nightmare."

I laughed. "I'll be sure not to give them anything not pre-approved."

Parker and Noah headed to the bar to pour us drinks, and I sat down with the women while the men turned their attention back to the grill. I listened as the conversation flowed from sleep training techniques to what preschool was best. I felt a little left out—was I the only one here without kids?

The guys returned with drinks for us—something nonalcoholic for Ava, which no one picked up on—and they brought more people with them.

"Look who we found," Noah announced.

A man with red hair and a blonde woman with freckles and big eyes appeared.

Behind them, Gavin Austin followed.

I knew it was him—I would know that face anywhere after I'd seen him on TV—and I'd thought all kinds of very dirty things about him.

My cheeks colored, and when he greeted me, taking my hand, I blushed even harder. He frowned, but it changed into a smile.

"It's nice to meet you, Paige." His voice was deep and smooth, like velvet, and I melted a little. He looked over my shoulder. "Wow, you guys have a lot of kids."

Parker laughed. "The more the merrier, right?"

Gavin nodded and glanced at me. "Are any of those yours?"

I shook my head. "No kids."

He looked visibly relieved. "Yeah, me either." He lowered his voice. "I never know what to say to them."

"The kids?" I asked.

"No, the parents."

I looked toward the group of people. "I thought they were your friends."

"Well, yeah. When the kids are around, though, they go into parent mode, and then it's all about good manners and low sugar and bedtime's at eight... or something."

I laughed. "Yeah, I got that, too. The moms were all talking about the latest trends in kids' clothes and what themes to do for parties this year. Lexi said something about doing a sugar-free party."

"She doesn't have kids, does she?" Gavin said with a frown.

I laughed. "No, I don't think so."

"She might change her mind once she has kids. I've heard sometimes, you just throw candy at them and run."

I burst out laughing. "You're going to be a great father one day, I can tell."

"It's in my genes," Gavin said with a smile.

I giggled and sipped the chilled white wine Noah had brought me.

"So, when you're not giving out unsolicited parenting advice, what do you do?" I asked.

Gavin blinked at me. "Really?"

I glanced around. "Yeah? I mean... is it an inappropriate question?"

"No," he said with a laugh. "People usually know everything about me, so it's a breath of fresh air to be asked that."

"Oh, I don't know who you are," I said. "I mean, I've seen your face on the news..."

"Lovely," Gavin said dully.

"...but I don't know anything about you except that you're tall, dark, and handsome, and children scare you a little bit."

The moment the words about his looks left my mouth, I blushed.

"Tall, dark, *and* handsome, huh?" Gavin asked with a grin.

"Well, that's just my powers of observation speaking."

Gavin laughed.

What the hell was I saying? At least he seemed to enjoy it.

"Logistics," Gavin said. "My company, Core Innovations, specializes in import and export."

"Oh, that sounds interesting."

"No, it doesn't. It's really boring."

I laughed. "Then why do you do it?"

"Oh, I love it. I'm also good at it, and someone once told me that it's the key to success. They were right."

Gavin smiled at me, and butterflies erupted in my stomach. He really was handsome, but when he talked, his mouth was mesmerizing. What would it be like to kiss him?

I flash back to my fantasy, with him on top of me, naked, buried inside me.

"What do you do?" Gavin asked.

You, if I'm lucky.

"I manage an administrative department," I said, sounding a lot more collected than I felt. My skin was on fire, and I was painfully aware of Gavin's lips. God, was the wine already doing a number on me?

We talked about my job for a little while before we joined the rest of the group. We chatted and laughed and drank—some of us more than others—and I had a lot more fun than I'd thought I would. The food was spectacular, too.

Bas apparently was the barbecue master.

When the clock struck nine, Ava yawned.

"I think that's us," she said. "We should get Warner in bed."

The other parents all agreed that it was time to pack the kids up and go, and a mass exodus happened where everyone collected their particular toddlers, said goodbye, and packed sleepy kids into their cars.

Finally, it was just me and Gavin, and Ryan and Samantha left on the lounge chairs. Emily had gone to put her kids to bed, and Parker was deep in conversation with Noah. Ava was holding a sleepy Warner off to the side.

"What are you guys going to do?" Ryan asked. "We want to go downtown, maybe hit a club."

"I'm not going out," Gavin said.

Ryan nodded. "Yeah, maybe that's a good call, given your situation." He looked at me. "It was very nice to meet you, Paige."

I said my goodbyes to him and Samantha, and they left.

"So, I guess it's goodnight, then," I said to Gavin.

"Oh, you're leaving?"

"No, I thought you were. You said you're not going out..."

"Yeah, it's better for me to stay out of the public eye right now. But I can hang out privately, in someone's home." He glanced at Parker, who was saying goodbye to Noah. "Maybe not this home, though. Do you maybe want to come to my place? I have drinks, and I even think there's still food in my fridge."

I laughed. "You think?"

Gavin shrugged. "It's anyone's guess. We can find out together."

I was still laughing. "Okay, yeah. That sounds great. Better than being in bed at nine thirty. I'm pretty sure that's where Noah and Ava are headed." I looked over at Ava, who yawned again.

Gavin nodded, and I walked over to Ava.

"I'm going to hang out with Gavin for a while."

"Yeah?" Ava asked, and her eyes sparkled.

I nodded, unable to hide a smile.

"That's a great idea. You should let your hair down a little. And, you know... use protection."

I laughed. "Thanks for that. I'll see you later."

"I'll text you our door code, and I won't wait up."

I walked back to Gavin, blushing bright red at Ava's statement.

After thanking Parker and Emily for hosting us, we left in Gavin's Porsche—of course someone like Gavin would drive a Porsche—and he drove through the glittering streets of LA.

6

Paige

"The city is incredible," I said, staring at the lights as we slid through the streets.

"I've always loved it here," Gavin said. He glanced at me, and his gaze was hot in the dark car. "There's something magical about this place. I always feel like anything is possible."

"Yeah," I said. That was exactly how LA felt to me, too.

Gavin put his hand on my thigh. The motion was natural, comfortable. We didn't know each other that well, but something about the evening made it feel like we'd known each other for a long time. Maybe it was just the wine that flowed freely through my veins.

I'd had more than I should have had. My head was light, and I felt warm and comfortable in my own skin.

Or maybe it was Gavin who made me feel that way. He had an easy way about him. Conversation flowed, and he was delicious to look at.

We arrived at a high-rise, and Gavin drove into the basement, parking in a spot that had his name on it. Two other cars were also lined up—a Lamborghini SUV and an expensive-looking BMW.

"These are both yours?" I asked, gesturing to the other cars.

Gavin nodded. "I didn't want to go all out, so I keep these three."

I giggled. He didn't want to go all out?

Gavin gestured for me to follow him to the elevator. When the doors slid shut, I was aware of the close quarters. Gavin stood close to me, and his hand brushed against mine. My skin tingled at the contact, and a shiver ran down my spine.

I felt him look at me, so I glanced at him. His eyes were dark.

"What?" I asked, my cheeks coloring.

"You're beautiful."

I smiled, my cheeks turning redder. "You're not too bad yourself."

He chuckled. "You really know how to stroke a man's ego."

I shrugged nonchalantly, although my insides were on fire. "I don't think you need a lot of stroking. You seem to know exactly what you have and that it's going for you."

"Oh, yeah?" Gavin asked with a grin. "You think I have something going for me?"

I chuckled softly and turned my head forward. Gavin made a move. He put his hand behind my neck, fingers tangling in my hair, and kissed me. The kiss was out of the blue, and I yelped softly, but I kissed him back. I'd wanted to kiss him all night. His mouth was incredible. I'd figured he'd be a good kisser, but *fuck*.

When he broke the kiss, my breathing was shallow and erratic, and I rolled my lips together.

The elevator doors slid open on the top floor, and Gavin led me to a front door—the only front door in the small hallway in front of the elevator. He owned the entire top floor of the building. It shouldn't have surprised me.

When Gavin opened the door, he let me walk in first and closed the door behind me.

"Can I get you something?" he asked.

I turned to face him. We stood close to each other—so close a sigh could have pushed us together. I was aware of the heat rolling off him.

I nodded.

"What can I get you? Something to drink?"

"I *am* thirsty."

His eyes slid to my lips. "So, what do you want?"

"You," I said in a breathy voice.

"This isn't why I invited you here—"

"I know." It was nice that he was a gentleman, but his kiss had only fired me up, and I wanted him. Badly.

Gavin's eyes locked on mine, and he took in what I'd said. He leaned forward and kissed me again, hand on my neck, his fingers playing with my hair when his tongue slid into my mouth. I moaned softly at the back of my throat, and Gavin's other hand slid down my spine toward my ass. He squeezed my ass cheek and pulled me even closer to him. Our bodies were pressed tightly together, my breasts mashing against his chest.

Gavin grinded his hips against me, and I felt his erection, hard and eager, in his jeans. The urge to have him inside me flushed through me, and heat pooled between my legs. I shivered and moaned again.

Gavin let go of my ass and found the hem of my shirt. He slowly worked it up my body while he kissed me. I broke the kiss and lifted my arms so he could pull it off. When I stood in my bra in front of him, he took the time to stare. I'd worn a black lace bra, and I had matching panties on, too.

"I like this," he said, tugging at the strap of my bra.

"You have good taste," I joked.

"It looks fantastic on you." His hazel eyes locked on mine again. "It'll look fantastic on my floor."

My stomach tightened, and Gavin kissed me again. He unclasped the bra expertly with one hand and tugged it off my shoulders. When he dropped it, we both looked down.

"Perfection."

I giggled.

Gavin's hands moved to my breasts, and he massaged them. My nipples hardened in his palms as he worked his magic. He moved in for another kiss and gently nudged me so that I stepped back until my back was against the wall. I gasped at the cold against my bare skin, but Gavin moved his head to my neck, and it distracted me. He worked his way down my neck and onto my chest, and I moaned.

When he kissed the delicate skin on my chest, Gavin moved a hand between my legs and cupped my sex. His hand was hot through the material of my leggings. He sucked my nipple into his mouth at the same time, and I whimpered, tilting my head back against the wall.

"It's like you're not wearing anything at all," Gavin mumbled against my breast.

"If you take them off, it will be true."

Gavin chuckled. He didn't pull them off right away—he was occupied with his mouth on my nipple, and I didn't want him to stop. He pulled the elastic band away from my hips and pushed his hands between my legs again, his fingers on the lace of my panties.

"Hmm," he said. His fingers pressed against my clit through the rough material, and I widened my stance to give him better access. "You're soaking."

"Wine makes me horny." I gasped.

"You make me horny," Gavin replied.

I closed my eyes when he moved to my other nipple, and his fingers rubbed the rough lace against my clit. The sensation made me shiver. Desire spread through my body as he paid attention to two erogenous zones at the same time.

I pushed my hands into his thick dark hair and whimpered and moaned as he pushed me closer and closer to the edge.

Gavin straightened, letting go of my nipples, and he looked me in the eye. With two hands, he pulled my leggings down. I scissored my legs, helping him get rid of the leggings and stepped out of them when they bunched around my ankles. He'd pulled my panties down with them, and I was naked.

"You look fantastic naked," he said in a thick voice, his eyes dark with lust.

"Let's even the playing field," I said. "You're still dressed."

I reached for Gavin's shirt and pulled it over his head, too. I took a moment to stare at him just as he'd stared at me. God, was it possible for a man that handsome to be so chiseled, too? Where the hell did they make men like him? He looked like he'd just stepped off the cover of *GQ* magazine. He was an Adonis, perfectly created for mortals like me to drool over.

I rolled my lips together again to make sure I wasn't actually drooling.

Gavin kissed me. My naked breasts pushed up against his bare chest. He wrapped an arm around my waist, and while he kissed me, he guided us toward the dining room table. I hadn't had the time to take in his apartment, but I got the feeling it was a large open-plan space.

When Gavin lifted me onto the edge of the table, he pushed me backward so I lay down. He ran his hands down my body and ran his fingers down my slit. I moaned and writhed when he flicked my clit.

He sank to his knees and pressed his mouth against my pussy, kissing me. I cried out when he stuck out his tongue and flicked it over my clit. I squirmed as he licked me harder and faster, and when he sucked my clit into his mouth, I cried out and arched my back, bucking my hips forward.

He took the invitation for what it was and lapped faster, licking, sucking, tasting. I moaned and whimpered and cried out as he pushed me closer and closer to the edge. When he moved down, he buried his tongue in my wet heat, and I moaned loudly. He licked his way up my pussy again, and I squirmed, pushing myself up against him.

He gripped my hips with both hands.

"Lie still," he ordered.

It was hard to do as he said, but I fought the urge to squirm, my body jerking involuntarily as he focused his attention on what he was doing. His tongue circled my clit, and I shivered. I was getting closer and closer, but Gavin drew it out, teasing me. My body grew numb, and the muscles at my core clenched. A primal being of pure lust woke up inside me. I ached for release. I ached for Gavin to fuck me.

He didn't let me orgasm. He took his time, licking and sucking my clit, flicking his tongue over it.

While he did that, he pushed one finger into me and then another. My eyes rolled back, and I closed them, giving myself over to the sensation. Gavin slowly pumped his fingers in and out of me, stroking my insides while he licked me, and it pushed me closer and closer to orgasm. Pleasure grew inside me, a live thing. It started off small, a flame that he slowly coaxed into a roaring furnace. I was hot, my legs felt like jelly, and my body jerked involuntarily.

He flattened his tongue, licking me from the base of his fingers to my clit, and that pushed me over the edge.

I cried out as the orgasm shattered through me. Gavin slowed his licking, but he kept up with his fingers, thrusting them into me along with the way my body contracted, clamping down on him. I gripped his hair tightly and pulled him closer to me, bucking my hips. Heat flooded my body, and I gasped for breath.

"You're so fucking hot," Gavin said.

I tried to remember how to breathe and swallowed hard. I was still reeling from the orgasm when he took my hand and pulled me up. He kissed me, and I unbuckled his jeans. He helped me, pulling his pants down. He took out his wallet when his pants got stuck and then kicked them off.

I stared at his cock, thick and large, standing at attention. The tip was slick with lust.

I wrapped my fingers around his cock, and Gavin sucked in his breath through his teeth. He opened his wallet and took out a condom. When he ripped the foil, I let go of him, and he rolled the condom over his cock before he grabbed my ass and pulled me closer to him. When he pressed against my entrance, I gasped, and when he slid into me, I moaned until he was buried inside me.

The feeling of him inside me was incredible. I trembled around his cock, filling me up, and Gavin's breathing came in shallow gasps. He held onto my ass and rocked his hips back and forth, sliding his cock in and out of me. It felt amazing, and I wrapped my arms around his shoulders.

"This isn't going to work," Gavin said.

"What?"

He lifted me off the table, and I wrapped my arms around his neck.

"I want to fuck you right." He carried me through his apartment. I kissed him, and I was only vaguely aware of the sheer size of the room and large windows.

Gavin walked me into a bedroom and climbed into a large bed with me. He all but fell into me, and I cried out.

"Better," he said, bucking his hips, sliding his cock in and out of me.

"Yeah," I said, but he took my breath away when he pounded into me harder and harder. I held onto his shoulders, the muscles rippling under my fingers as he held himself up with his arms on either side of my head, and I moaned in rhythm with our fucking.

Another orgasm grew inside me. His cock was enormous, and it rubbed up against all the right places. Pleasure grew inside me again, and in no time, I came undone at the seams. I fell apart and cried out before the orgasm took my breath away.

Gavin kissed me, swallowing my mewls and whimpers as the orgasm rocked my body.

When I came down from the orgasm, I looked at Gavin. His hairline was wet with sweat, and he was breathing as hard as I was.

"Lie down." It was my turn to do some of the work.

Gavin didn't wait for me to tell him twice. He pulled out and rolled onto his back. He put his hands on my hips and guided me onto his lap. I straddled his hips and sank onto his cock. I moaned as he penetrated me again, and Gavin groaned in unison.

He was buried deep inside me, and I shivered. When I rocked my hips, I felt him rearrange my insides. I bucked my hips back and forth harder and faster.

Gavin's brows knitted together, and he breathed hard through parted lips. His hands rested lightly on my hips, and I rode him hard. I wanted him to orgasm. My breasts jiggled, and Gavin stared at them for a moment before his eyes locked on mine again.

My efforts didn't only push him closer to the edge—I worked on my own orgasm, too. My clit rubbed against his pubic bone, the friction creating another wave of pleasure that built and swelled inside me.

After a couple more thrusts, I spilled over, orgasming another time. I leaned forward, collapsing onto Gavin's chest. He wrapped his arms around me and bucked his hips, fucking me from beneath when my orgasm stopped me from keeping the rhythm. His strokes were short and fast, and he bit out a cry in my ear, thrusting himself into me as deep as he could go. I felt him pulsating and throbbing as he released, and it prolonged my orgasm.

Finally, after the orgasms faded, I rolled off him. We lay side by side, trying to catch our breath.

He looked at me and grinned.

"Good end to a night, huh?"

"Ended it with a bang."

He laughed and shook his head.

"I'll be right back," he said and walked to a door that led to a bathroom. I sat up on the bed and looked around. All my clothes were in the living room. When Gavin returned, he was sans condom. I stood from the bed.

"I'm going to get dressed and go if that's okay."

"Of course. I don't expect you to stay the night."

"Not if it's just a one-night thing, right?"

"Right," he said with a grin, and he really looked okay with it. I was relieved—this couldn't be something emotional. We couldn't cuddle and talk and get attached. I was going home in less than a week, and our paths wouldn't cross again.

I walked to the living room, found my clothes, and pulled them on. Gavin followed me a moment later, wearing boxers.

He leaned against the doorpost, arms crossed over his chest while I hooked my bra and pulled on my top. I fluffed my hair.

"I called my driver. He'll take you back."

"In the middle of the night?"

Gavin nodded. "I pay him a shit ton of money to be at my beck and call. He doesn't mind." Gavin walked to me and pulled me in, planting a kiss on my lips. "It was really good meeting you, Paige."

I smiled. Everything about Gavin was so easygoing. There was nothing awkward about what had just happened and the fact that I was leaving. We were just two people who had had fun together, and the night was over now.

"It was great meeting you, too."

Gavin opened the front door for me and waited while I summoned the elevator. When I stepped in, I looked at him one more time. He grinned at me and winked, and the door slid shut.

7

Gavin

"Good morning, gentlemen," I said with a broad smile when I walked into the conference room. "It's a good day to make money." I rubbed my hands together.

The director and two investors of Newmark & Lewis sat around the conference room table wearing poker faces. I had no idea what they were thinking or what kind of mood they were in.

Newmark & Lewis was largely a conservation company serious about going green. They'd started off as an investment company, but when Gordon had upgraded his buildings, making them more "green," the public response had been so overwhelmingly positive that they'd decided to change their direction. I was interested in getting involved with them for the sake of bringing the green image to the forefront and making my own company more trustworthy in the eyes of consumers.

Eco-friendly was the name of the game, and the only way to stay on top was to keep up with the times.

"Let's get started, shall we?" I said brightly. "If everyone is ready with coffee, water, something stronger?" I looked around with a grin.

When they stayed straight-faced, my smile faded, and I cleared my throat. Maybe the "something stronger" joke had been too much.

"I think we're ready to get going," the director, Patrick Gordon, said.

His two investors, Hector Margate and Sean Humphrey, both nodded. They didn't have anything to drink in front of them. Not those kinds of people, then.

It was fine, I could deal with this. This was my job, my company. I'd started from scratch and worked my way up to millions and billions of dollars. I knew what I was doing.

"Right. I trust you received the paperwork my associate sent you?"

They all nodded.

"You're well up to date on what the company has to offer in terms of revenue. Not to mention that you'll be attached to the company name. Core Innovations has always been associated with positive influence and hope for a brighter future. Now, if we look at the numbers, you'll see that—"

"Let's talk about that," Gordon said, interrupting me.

"What?" I asked with a frown.

"The company name." Gordon nodded.

"Okay," I said, unsure. The name of the company had always been a good one, and as far as mergers and business deals were concerned, it wasn't usually the point of discussion. I liked to focus on numbers—that was what investors and collaborators were interested in.

"You say Core Navigations has always been associated with a positive influence, but in the light of most recent news, I'm not sure that's true."

"What do you mean?" I asked, confused. "The company has never faltered. I'm serious about what we do here, and—"

"I'm not talking about the company," Gordon said. "I'm talking about your relations with Tara Logan."

My stomach dropped, and I clenched my jaw. "My personal life and the company name have nothing to do with each other."

"We disagree," Humphrey said, speaking up for the first time. "You're the face of the company."

Margate chimed in. "Usually, we're not too worried about the tabloids and celebrity gossip. Celebrities and the business world only rub shoulders now and then, and it's not usually something to be concerned about, but considering your family history..."

He didn't have to finish the rest of his sentence. He was talking about the fact that my dad was an alcoholic, and Tara had made it sound like I was one, too.

"Gentlemen, please," I said, forcing myself to remain calm and professional. My pulse raced, and blood rushed in my ears. I was getting pissed off at Tara all over again. It had been a couple of weeks since the breakup, and she was still fucking shit up for me. "Don't let the slander of a scorned lover blind you to what a good thing this business deal can be."

"We're worried about how it might come off to the public. We focus on green and clean energy, but along with that, we believe in a moral compass, and our values are important to us. It goes against the company image to hitch our wagon to a company where there are so many gray areas."

"What gray areas?" I cried out. My control was slipping. "I am not my father, and I'm not the person Miss Logan is making me out to be. My company has a good reputation. The proof of the pudding is in the eating! Our turnover every quarter is incredible, our shares sell for prices that shoot through the roof, and the work we do every day is a testament to how successful Core Innovations is. You're willing to let that slip through your fingers because of what one woman is saying?"

My brow broke out in a sweat, and I felt hot. I fought the urge to tug at my tie. I was getting angrier and angrier, and it was tough to keep calm and steady.

Gordon shifted in his seat and glanced at his investors. Something wordless passed between them, but it didn't take a psychic to know it wasn't positive.

"Unfortunately, we're not going to do business with you at the moment," Gordon said simply. "The decisions I make for Newmark & Lewis are at my discretion, and our message doesn't align with yours."

"That's a load of bullshit!" I cried out, unable to keep my frustration away. "You want to make money, I want to make money, and together we can do that. It's the only *message* you should be worrying about right now! I didn't spend so many weeks of my time preparing documents and ledgers for you to look at just to have it thrown back in my face! You're cowards, all of you!"

Gordon raised his eyebrows, and the three of them stood, buttoning up their blazers.

"I think we're done here."

I shook my head and pinched the bridge of my nose between my thumb and forefinger.

"Let's talk about this," I said, trying to reel in my anger.

"I think we've heard what we needed to hear," Gordon said tightly.

They headed toward the door, and I put my hands on my hips and sighed. When they were gone, I sat down in the chair behind me, stretching my legs out. I tilted my head back and groaned.

Tara was fucking everything up for me. She'd brought in my family, my personal life, and now my business was suffering under it.

"Sir?" Dana, my secretary, asked. "I thought you were long done with the meeting."

"I am." I sat up. How long had I been sitting here? "What can I do for you?"

"Miss Logan is here to see you."

"Really?"

Dana nodded. "She won't budge. I told her you wouldn't want to see her, but she's determined, and she's been in the lobby for two hours. I think she's going to stay there until security physically drag her out." Dana worried her bottom lip. "What should I do?"

"I'll take care of it." I ran my hands through my hair. I had a bone to pick with her, anyway.

"Are you sure?"

I nodded and stood.

"Yeah, send her to my office."

Dana disappeared, and I walked to my office. I shrugged out of my blazer, loosened my tie, and rolled up my sleeves to my elbows. I'd dressed to the nines in a three-piece suit to meet with the guys from Newmark & Lewis, and it had blown up in my face, anyway.

My office door opened, and Tara walked in.

"Gavin," she said with a smile. She looked emotional. "It's so good to see you."

I turned to face her, hands in my pockets. She took a few steps closer like she expected me to hug and kiss her. When I didn't move, her steps faltered.

She looked good—Tara had always been a blonde bombshell. Her shoulder-length blonde hair was wavy, and she wore smokey makeup that brought out the blue in her eyes. She wore a tight pink dress that hit her above the knee. It was classy, not too revealing. Tara had always taken care of her looks. Other reality show stars came across as slutty sometimes, but Tara was all class.

It was her personality, her game of seduction, that gave her the edge.

"What do you want?"

She looked taken aback by how short I was.

"I just thought we could talk. We never really talked when you ended things."

"There isn't anything to say."

"You can't mean that," she said softly. "Three years together can't end like this, with nothing between us at all. We had a good thing, Gavin."

"Yeah?" I asked and walked to my desk, putting an object between us. I sat down, and Tara followed my lead, taking a seat in one of the armchairs facing me. "You're going out of your way to make me look like shit to the public. Don't talk to me about having a good thing."

"I know it was wrong," she said, looking down at her nails. "I was just so angry. Hurt. You just dumped me, Gav. What was I supposed to do?" She turned her bright-blue eyes up at me, and they were filled with tears.

I stared her down. I wasn't going to fall for her manipulation. She could cry all she wanted; she'd just lost me Newmark & Lewis. My sympathy for her was nonexistent.

"Don't you see that I love you? I've always loved you. I don't understand what's happening."

"You loved the idea of me."

"That's not true," she said, and her tears rolled down her cheeks. She wiped them away quickly, as if she were embarrassed that she was crying, but I knew it was part of the act. "You were my everything... you still are. Can't we try again?"

"I don't know, Tara. It's so hard for you to have to date me, to be in a relationship with a man when you're not the only one... you have to compete with my drinking for my attention."

She pursed her lips and nodded. "You're right. I shouldn't have said that. You were just so distant, so unavailable. All I wanted was to talk, to see if we couldn't work it out."

"So, you thought slandering my name would drive me back into your arms?"

"I was reeling, shocked, I wasn't thinking straight," she said. "You don't know what it is when love drives you crazy."

"I don't think love did that," I said tightly.

Tara shook her head. "I know this was a mistake. We belong together, and I won't stop trying to win you back. You'll see, in time, you'll figure out that we're meant to be. I'll wait for you until you're ready. I won't give up on us."

I shook my head. "Give up on us, Tara. It's not going to happen."

She stood. "Whatever it is you're going through, I'll let you figure it out. I'll be here when you're ready, okay? I'll always love you."

I groaned. "Don't do this. You're just making it harder for yourself."

Tara turned her head to the window. "You know, I've never really understood you. I guess that's part of what I love about you—your mystery. They say you don't know what you have until it's gone, and they're right. I know now what I had, and when we're past this rough patch, I won't make the same mistakes as before."

"Tara," I said, but trying to convince her it was pointless wouldn't work.

"I'll give you space to breathe, and then we can talk again," she said and walked to the office door. "Thank you for seeing me. You have no idea how much it means to me."

She opened the door and left, and I shook my head.

Damn it! I wished she would just let it go. I hated that she was spreading rumors about me—it affected my life in all the wrong ways—but having her tell me she was going to wait for me was a lot worse.

I just wanted her to move on with her life so that I could, too.

There were much better women out there, better suited to me and what I needed. If anyone had shown me that, it was Paige. She was the kind of woman I could just be myself around. She was nothing like Tara.

The problem was she was all the way on the other side of the country.

I sighed. What had I done in my life to deserve this fucked up mess?

8

Paige

I walked into the pub and looked around.

"Over here," Gina called, and I smiled and waved before walking to the table.

Gina and Cat, two of the women who reported to me in the office, had invited me out for drinks. I hadn't wanted to join them at first—I didn't know them very well—but they were making an effort, and since Ava had left, I'd been in limbo when it came to friends.

Maybe I could find someone new to hang out with. It wouldn't be the same as with Ava, but it was worth a shot, right?

"You worked late tonight," Gina said when I sat down. She took the hair tie from around her wrist and pulled back her dark curly hair into a bun.

"Yeah, I had to take care of a couple of things."

"You're so dedicated," Cat said. "I don't think I'll ever feel so committed to my job."

"That's why you haven't been promoted in three years," Gina said and bumped Cat, who rolled her eyes before they burst out laughing.

I smiled, but my insides were turning, and I felt sick. I pressed my hand against my stomach.

"Are you okay?" Cat asked.

"Yeah, I just feel off. I think it's something I ate."

"The cafeteria food at the office is shit. You shouldn't touch the stuff."

"I've never had issues before."

"It only takes once," Gina said gravely. "We usually go to Struben's, just down the road. Do you know it?"

I shook my head. I'd never heard of the place, and the name didn't make it sound very inviting.

"You should join us there for lunch next week," Gina suggested. "Their menu is very competitive."

Cat burst out laughing. "Do you hear yourself? What does that even mean?"

"Tell me I'm wrong," Gina challenged.

"You're not wrong, you're just weird," Cat said, and they bantered happily back and forth. They'd been friends for a long time, and it was clear they had inside jokes. They'd been nice to ask me to join them, but I felt like an outsider.

"What are you drinking?" Gina asked when she waved at a server.

"I don't know... just water for now."

"What?" Cat asked, perplexed. "When we invited you out for drinks, you know we meant alcohol, right?"

I laughed. "Yeah, but my stomach isn't feeling too great right now. Let me just get settled, okay."

"Wait, you're not pregnant, are you?" Gina asked.

I shook my head. "Of course not. I don't even have a boyfriend."

"Why don't you have a boyfriend?" Cat asked. "Is it because you work so much? It's a killer in relationships, you know. That's why I always take it easy."

"You're not even dating!" Gina cried out, and they laughed and joked again without waiting for an answer from me about why I wasn't dating.

Just as well, I hadn't known what to say. I wasn't dating because... I wasn't? I didn't have a list or a timeline or a specific reason. It was just the way it was right now.

The server came and took our orders, and I sat back and listened to the conversation.

"I think Johnny should introduce us both to his friends," Cat said after Gina had gushed about her perfect boyfriend. "Then, if we're all friends, we can do group dates and stuff. It will be so much fun!"

"Yeah, Johnny's brother Dave is recently single, and he might like you, Paige," Gina said, tilting her head to the side. "He's not hot, but he's not ugly, maybe a little weird looking... but he's got a great personality."

"Oh, that sounds—" I started, but Cat wouldn't let me finish.

"You're doing a shitty job selling him for someone who works in marketing."

"I'm not trying to *sell* him," Gina said with a laugh. "But she should know what she's getting herself into. Some frogs don't turn into princes when you kiss them, you know. They just stay frogs."

Cat shivered. "I hate that visual." She looked at me gravely. "Maybe you shouldn't go for Dave."

"He didn't do anything to deserve her rejecting him!" Gina cried out.

"I haven't even met him," I offered. "I'm sure he's a really nice guy, though."

"There we go," Gina said. "See? He's a nice guy."

I shook my head, and our drinks arrived. I was worried about Gina and Cat drinking—they were already all over the place, and that was sober. I hadn't seen this side of them in the office.

I sipped my water, and the conversation changed from princes and frogs to celebrity gossip.

"Did you hear another season of *FML* was announced?" Cat asked. "It's airing next month. I can't wait!"

"What's *FML*?" I asked.

Gina and Cat both looked at me like there was something wrong with me.

"It's a reality show called *Fuck My Life*. It's where people who go through really awful things talk about it and try to find people who will be there for them. It's like a psychology thing."

"Mixed with a game show."

"What?" I asked. "That sounds—"

"It's *so* fun to watch. I bet Tara Logan is going to be on it, too."

"Tara Logan?" I asked.

"Yeah, you know, the reality show star who dated that abusive guy."

I bristled. "He's not abusive."

Cat and Gina both glared at me.

"Of course he is," Gina said. "It's all over the news how he used her to make his image better because he can't do it himself. He used her, and then he dumped her, and she's just broken about it."

"Do you know her?" I asked carefully.

"Well, not personally, but who does?" Cat said. "I read up everything there is to know about her. She's my favorite reality star to date. She's so wholesome and down to earth. She doesn't deserve the shit she has to deal with every day."

They kept talking, but I switched off. I didn't want to hear how they thought Gavin was the villain. I didn't want to know how wonderful Tara was because none of it was true. Gavin was the sweetest guy. If I hadn't had to come back to Seattle, I would have liked to have seen him again.

My stomach rolled again. The water wasn't helping. Neither was the conversation. I got the feeling Gina and Cat were not going to become my best friends after all.

"I think I'm going to go," I announced.

Gina and Cat stopped talking.

"What?" Gina asked. "Why?"

"It's still early," Cat added.

"I feel really sick." It wasn't a lie. "I think I need to get to bed and sleep it off."

"Yeah, okay, I guess that's probably for the best…" Gina didn't sound happy, and I felt a little guilty for just leaving when they'd invited me out, but I couldn't do this for the whole night. They weren't exactly my people, and I was feeling worse and worse the longer I sat there.

"Thank you for inviting me. Have a fun night."

I took out some cash for my water and tip and put it on the table before I left. I got into my car, and my stomach lurched again. God, what a disaster.

On the way home, I called Ava.

"Are you awake?"

"It's still early, Paige," Ava said with a giggle. "Yeah, I'm awake."

I missed my friend so much. Her voice filled my car speakers as my phone connected to the Bluetooth while I drove.

"What have you been up to?" she asked. "Why aren't you out painting the town red? It's Friday."

I told her about my night with Gina and Cat.

"I really tried," I said after I'd relayed how the night had gone. "I tried so hard, but oh my God. I'm glad I feel sick so I could leave with a good reason."

Ava laughed. "It sounds terrible!"

"You should have been there." Then again, if Ava had been here, it wouldn't have happened in the first place.

"You're feeling sick?"

"Yeah, I don't know if it's something I ate. Maybe the chicken at the cafeteria... I usually love it, but lately when I have it, I just feel sick to my stomach. Maybe I'm off chicken now."

"Really? Paige, that's serious. You love chicken."

I shrugged. "People change, right?"

"Not that drastically." Ava hesitated for a moment. "Since when does chicken make you feel sick?"

"I don't know... the last couple of days?"

"When are you on again?"

"What do you mean?"

"You know, your period."

"Oh, I don't know. It should be soon. Um..." I tried to work out when my last period had been. When was it? Two weeks ago? Three? No, that didn't sound right. "I can't remember."

"Did you have one after you were here?"

"Why are you asking me that?"

"Because you're feeling sick and you have food aversions. That's pregnancy, my friend."

"What?" I cried out. "Don't be silly. I probably have food poisoning. It's not the same thing." I tried to convince Ava, but my mind was spinning. I *hadn't* had a period since I'd come back from LA, and I'd been there more than a month ago. That put me at almost seven weeks late.

Shit.

"I have to go," I said quickly. "I'm getting another call. It's my mom, and you know how she can be." It was a lie; I didn't have another call coming in.

"Are you going to be okay?"

"Yeah, fine. I'll call you later."

I ended the call and let out a slow breath, gripping the steering wheel with both hands.

There was no way I could be pregnant. We'd used protection.

My stomach twisted, and my mouth filled with saliva, the way it did when I was close to throwing up.

Shit, shit, shit.

When a wave of nausea hit me, I pulled to the side of the road and opened the car door, throwing up out of the car without even having time to unfasten my seat belt.

Oh God. I was in trouble, wasn't I?

When I was sure nothing else would come out, I shut my door and pulled into the road again. I stopped at a convenience store. The yellow lights from inside fell through the large windows onto the curb, and air conditioning ruffled my hair when I walked through the doors.

I found the aisle where they sold condoms and diapers and pregnancy tests altogether. Great. I glared at the condoms before I took a home pregnancy test off the shelf and walked to the checkout counter.

"Oh, honey," the woman behind the register said when she picked up the box to scan it. "What are we hoping for?"

"What?"

"Were you trying? You know, these things aren't always accurate. If you want accurate results, you should take a blood test, too."

"Thanks," I mumbled. It was none of her business.

"My daughter got three false negatives before she tested positive. She took so many of these things, I think it was by sheer strength of will that she ended up being pregnant." She laughed, and I smiled politely, paying for the test.

"Ginger tea."

"What?"

"It helps the morning sickness."

"I don't know if I'm pregnant yet." That wasn't true. I was pretty sure. A late period? Sickness? Aversion to chicken, like Ava had said...

"Good luck, honey. I'm crossing my fingers for you!"

I smiled and left the convenience store as quickly as I could just to get away from Ms. Optimistic. What was she crossing her fingers for? A positive? A negative?

When I arrived home, I went straight to the bathroom and peed on the stick. Two minutes felt like an eternity, and I tried to steady my nerves.

Breathe in, one, two, three. Out, one, two, three.

What was I going to do? What about work? What about Gavin?

God, I was pregnant. I knew I was. When Ava had said it, it had clicked into place, and... I picked up the stick to check the results.

Pregnant, but that was just a confirmation of what I already knew.

I threw the stick away, flushed the toilet, and washed my hands. I looked at myself in the mirror, and then suddenly, it hit me.

Pregnant. I was pregnant. Gavin Austin was the father, and I had a baby growing inside me.

Suddenly my throat tightened, and the nausea came back in full force. How the hell was I supposed to do this?

I covered my face with my hands and waited for some answer to come. It didn't. All I knew was that I was pregnant; the father was on the other side of the country, as was my best friend. I was completely alone.

Shit.

9

Gavin

When I knocked on my mom's door, she opened it wearing colorful layers of fabric with a scarf twisted around her hair. "Oh, wow."

"What do you think?" She turned around so I could see the whole look.

"It's very... eclectic."

She clapped her hands together. "Exactly what I was going for. Come in, come in." She beckoned me into the house, and I stepped in through the door. I'd bought her the modest house in the suburbs when I'd made enough money to be able to do it, cash. She deserved a good life. What my dad had done to her wasn't her fault, and it was good she'd left him behind and started over.

"What are you drinking?" Mom asked when we walked into the breakfast room. "I got ingredients for mimosas."

"It's ten in the morning, Mom. I'm not drinking champagne."

"Oh, okay," Mom said with a shrug. "We'll have the orange juice straight, then."

I laughed. "That sounds good." I looked at the table. "That's quite a spread."

Mom nodded. "I wasn't sure what you liked, so I got all of it."

The table was laden with pancakes, scrambled eggs and bacon, muffins, sausages, fruit, yogurt, and a variety of tarts and pies.

"You didn't have to do that, Mom."

"Of course I did. I don't see you all that often. Besides, it's my birthday. I get to go all out if I want to."

A pang of guilt shot into my chest. Mom didn't live that far away from me, but it was so easy to live past each other. I saw her on big holidays, Mother's Day, and her birthday.

"I got you something," I said and took a flat velvet box out of my backpack. Mom's eyes sparkled when I handed it to her.

She opened it up to reveal a diamond necklace and matching earrings.

"Oh, sweetheart, it's beautiful."

"It's called Dominique."

"What?"

"The necklace."

"It has a name?"

I nodded. "It's custom-made by a friend of mine who specializes in diamonds and pearls, and all his big pieces have names."

"Well," Mom said and lifted the necklace out of its box. I helped her put it around her neck. "Dominique and I are going to have a lot of fun." She laughed, and I grinned, glad to have made her happy.

"Eat something, honey, you're skin and bones," Mom said.

I rolled my eyes and picked up a plate to dish for myself from the large buffet in front of me. I wasn't skin and bones, I worked hard to look the way I did, and my suits were starting to stretch tighter around my biceps and thighs—I was doing something right. Ryan knew what he was talking about, even though he was reed thin. He didn't always practice what he preached, but he preached truth.

Mom served herself some food, too, and we ate.

"So, your father called this morning."

"Oh."

"He calls every year for my birthday. He has since the day I left."

I glanced at Mom. "As soon as he realized you were gone, you mean."

Mom tutted. "Don't be mean about it. We had our troubles, but that doesn't mean we didn't love each other. You should talk to him."

"No, I shouldn't. You can if you want to, but that doesn't mean I will."

"He's still your father."

"That doesn't mean jack shit. A father is someone who's there for you. He's just a sperm donor. I don't owe him anything," I shook my head. "Parents don't reserve the right to be friends with their kids for the rest of their lives. He didn't do anything to deserve it. In fact, he did the opposite. I don't have to do shit."

"Watch your language. There's no need to be crass."

I fought the urge to roll my eyes and pushed away the frustration that surfaced. This was why I didn't like seeing my mom. She talked about my dad all the time like he didn't fuck up our lives.

"How have you been?" Mom asked, changing the topic.

"I've been good. I'm struggling a little at work, but it's nothing too serious."

"I've seen you in the news a lot lately."

I nodded. "Yeah, it will blow over eventually. At least... that's what Melissa says. I don't know when it will happen. It doesn't feel like there will be an end to this."

"It will sort itself out, honey. Why didn't you tell me you and Tara were having trouble? She didn't know anything at all."

I sighed. Her opinion about our breakup was all over the news—everyone knew exactly how she felt about it.

Mom and Tara had been good friends from the day I'd introduced them to each other. I had a feeling Mom was more upset about the breakup than I could ever be.

"It's complicated, Mom. It wasn't really something I could talk about. It was just... a feeling."

Mom shook her head. "If you have something good, you fight for it, Gavin. I don't need to tell you that a good thing is hard to find."

"It wasn't that good, Mom. Really, it was better that I broke up with her."

"That's not what she says."

I frowned. "You still talk to her?"

"Well, yes. Did you think we would just stop talking to each other because you called it off with her? She's been a part of our lives for three years. That's a long time. She's like a daughter to me. At least... that's where I thought you were headed."

She'd been a part of our lives for too long, I thought, but I didn't say it.

"She doesn't agree with me, but it wasn't working for me," I said. I wanted to add that Tara had been nothing but a gold-digger, but if Mom still talked to Tara, I wasn't going to say anything that could cause shit when it got back to her. My mom had good intentions, but her execution wasn't always so great. She had a lot of flaws. I loved her, but sometimes she drove me crazy.

"Just think about what it all means," Mom said. "Maybe you acted too quickly."

"Or maybe, I should have done it a long time ago," I said hotly. "Seriously, Mom, you can't defend her after everything she's been saying about me."

"I'm not defending her. I don't think she's right, but people make mistakes. It's our job to forgive and forget."

"Yeah, I can forgive, but I won't forget. Going back to that is just stupid—you didn't think Dad was going to change either, so you left him, right?"

Mom pursed her lips. "It's not the same thing."

"It is. It didn't work, so I ended it. That's the crux of the story."

Mom sighed. "I just want to see you happy, honey. I know you haven't had the best example of a relationship, but I want you to find someone who can stand by your side."

For some reason, Paige flashed before me. I shoved the thought away—she'd been great, but I barely knew her. She'd been down to earth and a lot of fun, but she wasn't even in this state, let alone in town.

"If I find her, that will be great, but I don't think it's going to happen anytime soon, and I'm fine that way. I have the company, and that's enough."

If the company survived all the shit Tara was spreading about me.

The doorbell rang.

"Oh, I'll be right back."

"You're expecting someone?" I asked, but Mom didn't answer me.

I heard her open the door, and the other voice made my blood run cold.

Tara?

Mom led my ex-girlfriend into the breakfast room a moment later.

"Hi, Gavin," Tara said with a sweet smile. Mom carried a big bouquet of flowers.

"Look at what Tara brought me." She beamed. "I'm going to put this in water."

"Oh, no," I said and stood when Mom disappeared. "What the hell are you doing here?"

"I'm wishing your mom a happy birthday," she said. "I knew she was seeing you, and it's the only place I can get you to talk to me."

I stared at her. "Cornering me isn't a good way to start a conversation."

She rolled her eyes. "I'm not cornering you, Gavin. I just..." Her eyes shimmered. "I miss you."

I shook my head. "I'm not doing this. I'm out."

"You can't just leave. She'll be upset. You'll ruin her birthday."

"No, *you* will ruin her birthday." I picked up my backpack.

"Gavin, please," Tara said, stepping in front of me. "Could you just hear me out?"

I glared at her.

"Could you give me something?"

"What?" I was confused. "What do you want?"

"You kicked me out with nothing. I'm back living with my mom, and you know how I hate that. The least you can do is get me an apartment or something where I can deal with this media frenzy without—"

"You're asking for money?" I asked.

"I'm asking you to care, Gavin," Tara said. "You took back the credit card!" She swallowed hard, and when I didn't respond the way she needed me to, she changed direction. "You can't tell me you don't care. I don't believe, after all this time, you've just switched off and you feel nothing for me. We've been together for three *years*. Any other woman would get alimony, at l—"

"We weren't married," I said tightly.

"I gave up my apartment for you."

"I told you not to do that."

"Because you knew you were going to get tired of me?" Her eyes welled with tears.

"Because it was too soon," I clapped back. "I wasn't ready for that, but you wanted to be *together* for the sake of the press. That was what you said... it was just for the money, wasn't it?"

"I can't do this without you," she said. "You can't do this to me, make me face the sharks alone. I thought we were everything, Gav. I thought we were—" Her voice cracked, and she swallowed hard.

"Buy your own fucking apartment," I snapped.

"Just an allowance, then?" she asked. "A girl's gotta eat..."

Before I could respond, Mom returned with the flowers and put them on the table. She turned to us with a smile before her smile faded.

"You're leaving?" she asked, looking at the backpack in my hand.

"This wasn't supposed to be a group event."

"Gavin, don't do this," Mom said.

Tara looked at me with big eyes, but I shook my head. I walked to my mom and kissed her cheek. "I'll call you. Happy birthday."

When I turned, Tara stood right in front of me, blocking my way. I stared her down until she stepped out of the way.

"Don't ask my mom for money, either," I murmured hotly so only she could hear me, and then I left. I half-expected the paparazzi to be waiting for me in the road since Tara was here, but she wouldn't want them here if she wasn't being the blubbering victim. She'd come here to make demands, and no one could know about that. It would only ruin her sad victim image.

If they really knew what she was like...

When I got into my car, I let out a frustrated groan. No matter what I did, I couldn't get away from Tara.

Why the fuck was it so hard to get her out of my life?

I turned over the ignition and tried to decide where I was going. I'd told my mom no to champagne, but now I wanted a drink. I couldn't go anywhere, the paparazzi wouldn't follow me, and drinking at this time of day wouldn't do much to help my image.

Damn it, Tara had created a system where I couldn't do anything without being judged for it.

Instead of going to a pub, I headed toward Ryan's gym. If I couldn't drown my sorrows, I could try to physically run away from them.

It was the next best thing.

10

Paige

"I feel like we just did this the other day!" Ava said, wrapping her arms around me when I stepped into the terminal. Again.

"That's because we did do this the other day." I laughed. "Two months go by so quickly!"

"Much quicker when I know I'll see you again so soon," Ava said, letting go of me. "How are you feeling?"

We turned and walked through the airport together. This time, Ava had come to pick me up alone. Noah was at work, Warner was in preschool, and I was grateful to have my friend all to myself.

"I'm okay."

Ava narrowed her eyes at me. "Are you really?"

I glanced sidelong at her. "I don't know what else to say. I can't be anything but okay, you know? It's not like it will change anything."

Ava shook her head. "That doesn't mean you're not allowed to feel... whatever it is you feel."

I nodded. I'd told Ava about the baby soon after I'd found out. She was my best friend—I called her for anything from advice to secrets to the boring and mundane events of everyday life.

"I'm worried about what he'll say," I admitted.

After I found out that I was pregnant, it had taken me a while to figure out how I felt about it and what I wanted to do. It was a big thing to wrap my mind around. I wasn't sure I'd completely come to terms with it yet. I still had a lot of questions, but one thing I knew—Gavin had to know about the baby. I'd taken all the leave days I'd piled up over the years I hadn't taken a break. I hadn't thought I would dip into them again so soon, but this was important. My boss hadn't been happy, but I had accumulated days he couldn't argue with.

"I understand," Ava said. "I wish I could help you out and tell you how he will react, but I really don't know. I don't know Gavin that well. My friends here are still really new, and he's a friend of a friend, you know?"

I nodded. I'd hoped Ava could help me out, too, but the only way I was going to know how he felt was by talking to him.

"I think it's big of you that you're doing it face-to-face," Ava said.

We reached her car, and I loaded my bag into the trunk before climbing into the passenger seat.

"It's not the kind of thing you do over the phone," I admitted. "Besides, I don't have his number."

Ava turned over the ignition. "This whole thing is crazy," she said.

I sighed. "Tell me about it. I kept shying away from having some fun, just putting myself out there again, and now that I did... this happened."

Ava pulled into the road, and the city rose all around us as we drove to the suburbs of LA.

"It's going to be okay," Ava said. "Whichever way this goes. Have you thought about the different outcomes?"

"You mean if he doesn't want anything to do with me or the baby?" I asked. "Yeah, I have. I ran every scenario through my mind until I felt sick."

"Maybe it was just morning sickness."

I burst out laughing at Ava's joke.

"That's such a cruel thing to say."

Ava shrugged. "If we can't laugh about it..."

"We'll cry," I added with a sigh.

Ava smiled at me before focusing on the road again.

"Telling him is the right thing to do," I said, turning my face to the window. "He deserves to know. If he tells me he wants nothing to do with me, I'll go back to Seattle and figure it out. I can work my job around having a child. There are a million single moms out there who pull it off every day."

"And if he says he wants to be in your life, be a present father to the baby?"

I hesitated. "I don't know. That's the part where I got stuck."

We drove in silence for a while.

"If he tells me he doesn't want anything to do with the baby, it will be easy. It will be me and the baby, and I'll figure it out alone. If he wants to be in my life, I'm not sure how to manage it. With me in Seattle and him here..." I shook my head. "It will get infinitely more complicated from there. That's why I thought talking to him first was a good idea. After we talk, I'll know where we stand, and then I can take that next step."

"You've always been so logical," Ava said. "Even in really difficult, emotional situations, you always keep a clear head."

I nodded.

"What did your mom say?"

"I haven't told my family yet."

"What?"

"I know, I just wasn't ready. I need to know what's going on so I can be ready for whatever they throw at me. Mom will be happy about having another grandchild. I just need to know how I feel before I can take their comments."

"Your family can be a lot to handle sometimes."

I nodded. My family was loud and opinionated, and they weren't scared to speak their mind. It was fine when I knew what I felt—I could handle it when I was ready, and it was my choice. I just had to get to that point first.

We drove in silence the rest of the way. When Ava pulled into her driveway, she turned to me and took my hand, squeezing it.

"I know this is really crazy and it's going to be a rocky road ahead... but I'm so excited that we're pregnant together!"

I laughed and leaned over to hug her. "I'm glad you've already been down this road. You'll be able to talk me down from the ledge when I'm terrified and second-guessing myself."

"I'll be right here for it all," Ava said.

We climbed out of the car, and I took my bags into the house, getting settled in the same room I'd been in when I was here last. I fell backward on the bed. Everything felt so surreal. Some days, it was hard to think I was pregnant at all. Everything felt so *normal*.

It wouldn't stay like that forever. At some point, I was going to start showing, and eventually, I was going to have a baby.

God.

I was going to have a baby.

The rest of the day passed in a blur. Ava did a few things for work, fetched Warner from school, and we spent time playing with play-dough with him until Noah came home from the office.

When Noah arrived, I plagued him for Gavin's number and address so I could call him and arrange to see him. My stomach twisted into a knot of nerves when I dialed his number.

This was it. This was where my life—and maybe his, too—changed forever.

11

Gavin

Melissa walked into my office. I was sitting at my desk, my hands in my hair. Another article had circulated about me, this time in a business paper.

"It's spinning out of control," I said to Melissa when she sat down. "Did you see the *Fortnight*?"

The *Finance Fortnight* was a paper that circulated every two weeks with all the updates in the business world worth knowing. It covered everything from the stock market index to the who's-who to watch out for.

"I saw," Melissa said. She put her handbag on the floor next to the armchair she sat in.

"Since when is the *Fortnight* a fucking gossip channel? It's supposed to be about business, not about ridiculous made-up scandals." I blew out my breath, billowing my cheeks.

"If Newmark & Lewis released the statement, there isn't much we can do about it," Melissa said carefully. "People always thrive on gossip, and the paper's description doesn't exclude information like this."

I shook my head. "Well, it should." The article was about how Newmark & Lewis had decided to go in a different direction, not wanting to attach their name to mine. They could have just said they were planning something else; they didn't have to make it sound like I was the scum of the earth.

"I don't understand how this whole thing is spinning out of control," I said. "Tara shouldn't have this much leverage. She's a fucking reality show star! They're nothing in the world of celebrities."

"She's popular," Melissa said. "They love her, so whatever she says matters."

"Yeah? It shouldn't. Did I tell you she tried to call me again yesterday?"

"Did she?"

"I didn't answer. It's the third call I didn't take, which means at some point, she's going to arrive here again. I should put her on a persona non grata for the building."

"You can't do that."

"Why not?"

"If you treat her like she's a threat, it's going to blow up in the media. You know she's going to make a big deal out of it."

"So, what am I supposed to do?"

Melissa was quiet long enough that it made me worry.

"What?"

"You need to work on your image," Melissa said. "If you could find someone to move on with, someone who will make you look better..."

"No," I said. "You're asking me to just find someone to be with for the sake of getting rid of Tara? You think *that* won't make her lose her mind even more?"

"You have to fight fire with fire," Melissa said. "Be so good in public that you disprove whatever she says about you. Right now, she has the leverage because you're not showing your face in public at all."

"You told me to stay out of the public eye," I pointed out.

"I did, but now it's time to reintroduce you to the public as a changed man."

I snorted. "A *changed* man?"

"I know it sucks, but your public image is just a mind game. It doesn't matter who you really are—it doesn't matter who anyone really is. All that matters is what others think of you. It won't only affect your personal life, but your business, too."

I sighed. Melissa was right. I'd hired her to take care of my image for a reason. I just didn't always like the way she wanted me to do that.

"I'm going to get lunch," I said. "Are you going to stick around? I can get you something, too."

"If you don't mind me working here for a while, I'd like a sub from that new place on fourth."

"Sandwich Genie?"

"The one with the dumb name and the good food."

"Right," I said with a laugh. "I'll get you something."

I left the office. I had to get out and breathe. I felt like I was being trapped by all the stories, the gossip and the drama Tara created. The worst part was that she'd told me she'd been angry, but she didn't feel that way anymore. She'd stopped spreading rumors about me—they ran all by themselves now.

I headed toward the new place. It wasn't too far away from my office, and I enjoyed the walk. I loved the way LA lived and breathed all around me. The city had as much personality as the people who lived in it, and I loved being a part of the bigger picture. The city had a giant pulse, a life of its own.

My heart sank when I thought about the bigger picture. It could be good, and it could be bad.

Tara was fucking it up for me.

After getting sandwiches for me and Melissa, I walked back to the office.

"Gavin?" someone said just as I reached the door, and I turned.

"Paige?" I asked, confused for a moment before I remembered. "Oh, shit."

Her eyes widened in surprise at my exclamation.

"No, not 'oh shit' that you're here. 'Oh shit' I forgot we were supposed to meet. Fuck, I'm sorry."

She shook her head. "It's okay. I was just about to get into the car when I saw you. Is it a bad time?"

"No. I was just—"

"Gavin," someone else said, and I froze at the sound of her voice.

Tara walked up to us. Her eyes were trained on me, but they slid to Paige. I watched as Tara sized her up.

"Tara," I said tightly.

"Am I interrupting something?" Tara asked. "I was hoping we could talk. I've been trying to call..." She glanced at Paige again.

"Yes, I'm busy," I said formally. "I'm sorry, I don't have time to talk right now."

"It won't take long." She glanced at Paige again. "You haven't introduced me to your friend."

I searched for words and came up blank. It was none of Tara's business who and what—

"Girlfriend, actually," Paige said.

She glanced at me with a smile, giving me a pointed look. *Go along with it.*

"What?" Tara asked with a frown.

"I'm Paige," Paige said, holding out her hand. "Tara, was it?"

Tara nodded and forced a smile.

"Gavin hasn't mentioned you before," Tara said.

"He's very secretive," Paige said. "He hasn't mentioned you, either." She draped her hand over my shoulder, and I wrapped an arm around her waist, pulling her a little closer to me.

I caught a whiff of her perfume. She smelled *fantastic*.

Tara blanched at that, and I could have kissed Paige for being so great.

"Gavin," Tara said, her smile still on her face, but it didn't reach her eyes, and she looked like she was on the verge of hysterics. Her eyes were a little too wide, and she'd had enough meltdowns in our relationship for me to know all the tells by now. "I really need to talk to you."

"If you phone my secretary, I'm sure she'll find a space to squeeze you in," I said. "It's standard procedure." I needed her to know that she'd been demoted to someone who had to follow the right channels to get to me at all.

"You want me to talk to Dana?" Tara asked in a high-pitched voice. "She's for your *clients*. I'm not a *job*, Gavin."

"If you don't mind, we have a meeting to attend," Paige said. "It was nice meeting you."

Tara opened her mouth, sawed her jaw when she couldn't find the words and closed it again. Paige turned to the door and looked at me.

"Ah," I said and jumped forward to open the door for her before I stepped through it and into the building behind her. We walked to the elevator together, and by some miracle, Tara didn't follow us. I was sure she was still standing in the street, trying to figure out what had just happened.

"You're a saint," I said when we were in the elevator together, riding to my floor.

"She looks like a piece of work."

"You have no idea."

Paige chuckled.

When we stepped into my office, I introduced Paige to Melissa.

"Mel is my PR manager and the reason I still have some kind of reputation after this shitshow with Tara," I said. "She's a godsend."

Melissa laughed. "I'm just doing my job."

"You're doing it well," I said. "When Paige told Tara we're dating, she didn't know what to do. I thought she was going to cry." I laughed, shaking my head.

"Tell me about yourself, Paige," Melissa said.

"I'll make us coffee," I offered and gestured for Paige to sit down. "Please, make yourself comfortable."

I walked to the large coffee station in the corner and prepared three lattes.

While Melissa asked Paige about her life, I waited for the machine to produce the gourmet drinks. I listened as Paige explained what she did for a living, what her life was like in Seattle, what kind of family she came from… it took a while for me to realize what Melissa was doing.

"Here you go," I said, handing Paige a cup.

"Thanks," she said and sipped it.

"You're unattached?" Melissa finally asked.

"Well, no," Paige said with a grin. "Apparently, I'm dating Gavin, according to what Tara just found out."

"That's what I'm after," Melissa said. "You're not in a relationship, are you?"

Paige frowned. "What do you mean?"

"Well…" Melissa glanced at me.

"I want you to be my girlfriend," I said, getting where Melissa was going with this.

"What?" Paige asked.

"Just for now," I said. "It doesn't have to be real. I just want you to pretend to be my girlfriend for a while. I want to flaunt you to the big guys, show the world I'm not a bad person, and when all this is over, we can go our separate ways."

Paige blanched. "Gavin, I can't do that. I was hoping we could talk..."

"Please," I begged. "My market share value is going down, Tara is causing a whole lot of shit, and I need someone to pull me back up. That someone is you. I'll make this work for you, whatever you need. I can pay you for your time off work so you're not missing out on an income. I'll talk to your boss—you can even work for me, it will be like a work exchange, or something."

"Is that a thing?" she asked. She looked like a deer in headlights.

"I don't know. We'll make it a thing. You have all the right stuff." I sat down on the edge of my desk, my forgotten latte next to me. Melissa hadn't touched hers, either.

Paige clung to her latte as if it was a life preserver.

"The right stuff?" she asked in a small voice.

"A good family, a good career, a good reputation with nothing strange going on. You're a straightforward vanilla kind of girl," Melissa said. "And you're exactly what Gavin needs for his image right now."

Paige shook her head. I couldn't tell what she was thinking. She studied Melissa, and then she studied me.

"You have no idea how much you'll be saving me," I said. "I'll make it worth your while. It will be an adventure."

Paige swallowed hard. "I really need to talk to you," she said. "Alone."

"We'll have all the time in the world if we do this," I said. I stared at her, willing her to agree. I needed this—I *needed* Paige. I wasn't the best guy in the world to have as a boyfriend. I had a hell of a past, and work was my mistress, but Paige was independent, the kind of woman I could do something like this with. When I thought back to our night together, there had been no complications, no drama. Everything had been simple and straightforward, and we'd both known where we stood.

I needed that in my life.

"Okay," Paige finally said.

"Yeah?" I was surprised she agreed, but I was thrilled, too.

"Yeah," she said with a gasp. "I guess we can do it."

I grabbed her hand and squeezed it. "You have no idea what this means to me."

Melissa looked happy, too. This was what she'd wanted for me. I'd been against putting on an act, but this was different. This was with Paige, and with the kind of person I knew her to be, this was going to be fun.

"I have to go," Paige said, clearing her throat. "I have some planning to do."

"Right," I said. "Us, too. I'll call you later, and we'll talk, okay?"

"Oh," Paige said. "Yeah, that will be good."

She left my office, and I sank into my office chair.

"That was unexpected," Melissa said. "I think it will be good."

"Me, too," I said. "I didn't think anything about this thing with Tara could be good, but this..."

"She's a sweetheart," Melissa said.

I grinned at her. "Yeah, she is."

12

Paige

"How did it go?" Ava asked, coming to my room after I got back to the house.

I lay on my bed.

"Great," I said sarcastically. "We're dating."

"What?"

"It's not real, though. I'm his fake girlfriend until further notice."

Ava frowned and walked to the bed, climbing onto it. I let out a long sigh.

"I don't think a conversation could have gone any more wrong," I said and told her what had happened, from when we'd run into Tara to when I'd agreed to pose as Gavin's girlfriend.

The more I talked, the more Ava's eyes stretched until she looked as stunned as I felt by the time I was done with my story.

"Paige, this is insane," Ava said. "And you didn't tell him about the baby?"

"I couldn't! His PR manager was there. It's not the kind of thing I wanted an audience for. Besides, she went on and on about how perfect I was, with nothing ruining my name or my reputation. They both told me how good I would be for Gavin's image."

Ava shook her head as if she was confused.

"So, when are you going to tell him, then?"

"I can't tell him now," I said, scrubbing my hands down my face. "I'm supposed to be this saint with nothing bad in my life so that Gavin can look good. The last thing he needs for his image is a woman who's pregnant. If that comes out..." I covered my face with my hands and mumbled through my fingers, "I wish I hadn't jumped in and posed as his girlfriend to begin with." I lowered my hands. "She was just so possessive and demanding, and he was *so* uncomfortable, you should have seen him."

"That's one thing, but agreeing to be his fake girlfriend... ?" Ava asked.

"I know, I know." I fell back on the pillows. "You should have seen him, Ava. He was so desperate. I've been reading up on all this shit Tara is causing him after I knew he was the father of my baby, and it really is bad. The business is sinking because of this, and I couldn't just leave it. I was in a corner, and I panicked."

Ava shook her head again. "For someone as logical as you are, this is the most illogical thing you've ever done."

"I know." I groaned. "I don't know what I was thinking!"

"Tell him no," Ava suggested.

"I can't do that. I already gave him my word. Besides, Tara knows. It's already a hot topic, judging by how quickly gossip spreads when it involves her." I'd read all the articles about her, too. But I wasn't going to admit exactly how much digging I'd done on Gavin's ex. That would have suggested that I liked him.

Which I didn't.

Not more than anyone I'd slept with on a whim, although Gavin wasn't like other men...

"You're pregnant, Paige. You have to tell him at some point. You can't hide this forever. Eventually, he'll notice."

"Maybe it will be over by then," I said. "It can't last forever."

Ava gave me a pointed look, but she didn't get it. It wasn't just about the fact that his company was doing poorly because of this woman, and his image had been scathed. It was also the fact that Melissa had called me "straightforward vanilla." That was synonymous with *boring,* and fuck it, she wasn't wrong.

"Nothing in my life is exciting," I admitted to Ava. "Everything is always the same, predictable, and nothing ever happens. When he called it an adventure... I guess I just want something extraordinary to happen to me, you know? I just want something to give."

Ava pursed her lips. "Well, this isn't *ordinary*."

"No," I said with a laugh and pressed my fingertips above my left eyebrow where a headache was starting to form, "it's not."

Ava's face broke into a smile.

"What's so funny?" I asked.

"This whole thing," Ava said. "You have to admit, it's funny."

I giggled. "Yeah, I guess it is."

"In a really fucked up way."

I laughed and nodded. "Very."

We laughed together, and the tension left my shoulders. Okay, so my baby daddy was also now my fake boyfriend, and he didn't know I was carrying his child. I was helping him get rid of his ex-girlfriend, living a fake life in LA while my real life, with all its complications, waited for me in Seattle.

Everything was going to be fine, right? I just had to keep it a secret from Gavin—and the world—for long enough that his company was okay, have a fake breakup in public to end things, and then I could tell him and...

Then what? Would we ride off into the sunset together?

"Oh God," I said, pressing my hand to my forehead, and my laughter faded. "This is a mess."

Ava chuckled. "You can say that again. Do you know what will help, though?"

"What?" I waited for a snippet of divine wisdom from my best friend, whose life was so much simpler than mine.

"Ice cream."

"How does that help?"

"It doesn't, but it tastes good, and since you're eating for two, you can enjoy yourself a little without worrying that it will go to your hips. Come on. Warner is already asleep, so we don't even have to hide it."

I laughed. "Oh, the joys of parenting."

"You'll get there."

I wasn't sure how I felt about it. It was bad enough that I had this baby coming, which I still needed to wrap my mind around. Now, I had a whole new level to this game, and until recently, I hadn't even realized I was playing.

It was going to be fine, though. I just had to take this day by day.

One thing was for sure—my life was everything but boring now.

—ℓℓ—

"Welcome to *Metropolitan Prime*, where you'll find the latest celebrity news—and gossip—as it happens! I'm your host, Kieran Cohen, and joining me tonight is none other than Tara Logan!"

The audience erupted in cheers, and Kieran took his place next to Tara. She smiled brightly and waved at the applauding crowd.

"Now, Tara," Kieran said gently, "the last time we had you on the show, we had to cut it short."

"I was very emotional," Tara said, nodding. "It's tough to deal with, you know?"

"I can only imagine what you're going through. We're all so grateful you took the time to come back and finish the interview."

"Oh, it's the least I can do," Tara said with a smile at the audience again. "I know you're all so invested, and you all care so much, I can't just hide away."

The audience cheered.

"How have you been since we talked last?" Kieran asked.

"It's been tough, but I've been okay. It's not the first time I've had my heart broken, as you all know." She laughed, and Kieran nodded in agreement. "You'd think all those game shows would have prepared me for this, but the truth is, when it's real..." She got emotional and pressed her fingers to her lips.

Kieran reached for a tissue and handed it to her.

"Thank you," Tara said and dabbed the tissue to the corners of her shimmering eyes. "I just didn't think it could hurt that much, but that's what happens when you really open yourself up to someone. You make yourself vulnerable, and you hope and trust that he'll take care of your heart."

"He didn't do that, did he?" Kieran asked.

Tara shook her head. "I guess I should have seen the signs earlier, but when you love someone, you forgive their flaws."

"What flaws?" Kieran asked.

"I told you before it wasn't always perfect. Nothing is. I just didn't realize where I should have drawn the line. I loved Gavin. I still do—that will never change. I just wished I was the only person in the relationship with him."

"Weren't you?" Kieran asked, shocked, and the audience breathed in sharply and gasped, too.

"He would never have cheated on me," Tara said quickly. "It's just the drinking... it's hard to date someone when you don't always know which version of themselves they'll be. I say it like that because I realize now that it wasn't just me and Gavin. When he drank, he turned into someone else, and that man wasn't someone I knew or understood. It wasn't someone I could reach. It felt like everything I put into the relationship when he was drunk just poured into this black hole, never to be seen again."

"That must have been hard," Kieran said.

Tara nodded. "Exhausting is the word. There's only so much a woman can give before there's nothing left. I'm mourning the man I lost when we broke up—Gavin Austin will always be my forever, even if he doesn't feel the same way about me. But I don't miss the other guy, the man he becomes when he drinks. I guess in some ways, I should thank him for setting me free. I hope the woman he's with now has what it takes to deal with his troubled nature and to face the music when she has to deal with Mr. Hyde."

Kieran shook his head. "I'm hurt to know that you went through so much pain in silence when the world only saw your smile, but I'm so happy you're in a better place."

"I don't know if it's better yet," Tara said with a wan smile. "I lost a lot of good when I lost Gavin. I'm just trying to focus on what went wrong so that it will get me through and remind me that I'm better off." Her eyes shimmered again. "Even if it doesn't always feel that way." She sniffed and pressed the tissue against her nose. "I guess this is the nature of a toxic relationship, right?" she added in a wobbly voice. "No matter how bad they are for you, they've pulled you in so much you can't help but love them and ache when they're gone."

Kieran nodded sympathetically, and the camera panned away from Tara Logan, showing only Kieran Cohen's face.

"Straight from Tara Logan herself, the pain and pleasure that comes with love. Thank you for joining us on *Metropolitan Prime,* where we keep it real."

13

Gavin

"You look stunning," I said when I opened my front door to her looking like a vision. She wore the proverbial little black dress, but fuck, she wore it *well*. She had a great body. She clearly looked after herself; her skin was smooth, her hair was glossy, and she'd put on just the right amount of makeup—smokey but not caked on.

It wasn't just her body that made her irresistible. She had confidence, she was comfortable in her own skin, and she didn't look like she had something to prove to the world.

Confidence was the most beautiful thing a woman could wear.

"You clean up well, too," she said with a smile. Her green eyes were bright, and she hooked her light-brown hair behind one ear.

I chuckled. "Thanks." I'd put on a suit for the occasion.

"Are we ready to go?" Paige asked.

"Not yet. We don't have to be there for another hour. Come in."

She hesitated before she stepped into the house and looked around.

"I didn't notice how nice your place is the last time I was here," she said.

"No?"

"No. I was distracted."

I chuckled. Just thinking back to that night got me hot under the collar, and I tugged on my belt.

Paige walked deeper into the apartment. It wasn't very big, as far as apartments in LA went, but it screamed luxury. Emily had helped me decorate it after I'd bought it, but I wasn't home very often between work and traveling for work.

I tried to see it through a stranger's eyes, from the marble floors to the full-length windows that looked out over the nightlife of LA and the coastline, to the chandeliers that hung from the ceilings.

"Can I get you something to drink?" I asked. "I have wine, whiskey, vodka…" I walked to the wet bar that connected the living room to the next entertainment room. I studied the contents of the bar to see if I had something else to offer her. "Rum?"

"Oh…" She giggled. "No, thank you."

"Yeah, you don't strike me as a rum person." I grinned at her. "Wine, that's your drink? I have a really smooth vintage—"

"I don't drink."

I frowned. "You don't drink? I distinctly remember an alcohol-fueled night in this very apartment."

Paige's cheeks turned red. "I mean, I don't drink *anymore*. I think it's better if I don't, you know?"

"Why?"

She froze for a second. "For your image."

I blinked at her.

"If I'm going to be that girl that brings it all around for you, the *straightforward vanilla* girl, then I think it's safer if I don't drink at all."

"Huh," I said. "That's a big sacrifice to make."

"Oh, it's nothing," she said with a wave of her hand. "It's just a couple of months, right?" She swallowed and offered me a bright smile.

I smiled back at her. "Yeah, you're right." I put the alcohol down. "Why don't I get us something else? I think I have something in the fridge."

God, I sounded terrible when I said it that way. I didn't even know what nonalcoholic beverages I could offer her.

"Water is fine."

"You're sure?"

She nodded and walked to the kitchen. I poured us each a glass of ice water from the dispenser in the fridge and carried it back to the living room. I gestured for her to sit down. She made herself comfortable on one leather couch, kicking off her strappy heels.

"Do you mind?" she asked.

I shook my head. "Please, make yourself at home. You're going to be spending a lot of time here."

"I'm not complaining, this place is a palace."

I laughed and sipped the water, wishing it was vodka. Paige was beautiful. I'd already been tipsy when I'd met her the first time, and things had been so much easier. Without my liquid courage, I could be so awkward.

"Did you manage to get things straightened out with your boss?" I asked. "I can give him a call—"

"It's okay, I took care of it," Paige said.

"Okay, good," I said, nodding. "Thank you. For all of it."

"You're welcome."

"You said you wanted to talk to me about something the other day, and we never got around to it."

Paige paled a little. "Oh, it's nothing important."

"Are you sure?" I asked. "Isn't that what you came to see me for? When Tara interrupted us…"

"Some things seem important at the time, but then things change, and you realize it's not a big deal."

"Okay," I said. "You can talk to me about whatever, though. I know we're doing this thing, but I like to think that we're still friends after it all."

She smiled. "Sure. Friends."

The last thing I wanted to do was to fuck around with Paige on top of it all. She was doing me a huge favor, sacrificing a lot for me when she barely knew me. I wasn't going to mess with her by flirting, sleeping with her, and complicating things even more. Although, sleeping with her had been amazing the first time and if I had the chance…

I would let her take the lead on that, I decided. I wasn't going to say no if she offered, but I wouldn't ask. That seemed reasonable, right?

"Tell me about tonight," Paige said. "What should I expect?"

"It's a small event, closed, with only company members. My board of directors and investors are all going to be there, and a lot of my employees, but that's it."

"It doesn't sound very small. You have a large company."

I smiled. "How do you know?"

"I looked it up," she said simply.

"Yeah?" She'd looked me up? That was sweet. I hadn't realized she was interested.

"I figured if I have to pose as your girlfriend, I should know what's going on in your life when someone asks."

Right. Of course. Why wouldn't she look me up and find out about me when she had to pose as my fake girlfriend? This was a job, I had to remind myself. She was doing it to be nice, to play her role well. It didn't mean anything more than that.

"Are your colleagues very close?" Paige asked.

I shook my head. "I don't have any close relations in the company, except for Melissa. I'm very isolated, actually. My real friends are all outside the company."

"That seems very lonely if you work as hard as you do and spend so much time in the office."

I shrugged. "It's safer not to mix business with pleasure."

"Hmm, wise words," Paige said.

I glanced at the time. "We should get going."

We made our way to the basement parking, and I opened the door of my Lamborghini Urus for Paige. When we pulled into the road, I floored it, and the engine's power roared beneath us. Paige inhaled sharply. When I glanced at her, her face was riddled with pure pleasure.

"You like cars with power?" I asked.

"I love them," she said with a laugh.

I grinned, and we flew through the streets of the city. I broke a couple of road laws, going way too fast, but the look on her face was worth it.

When we pulled up in front of my office building, a red carpet had been rolled out, and two bouncers stood at the door with black suits and earpieces.

"Oh, this is fancy," Paige said. "A red carpet and everything."

"The company believes in going all out," I said. "It was Mel's idea to do this every year. I hate it, but it's good for my image, especially now."

"The *company* believes in going all out? Or you?"

"A bit of both." I chuckled.

"If your driving is any indication, I believe you." Her eyes danced with laughter.

I offered her my arm, and we walked into the building. We rode the elevator to the fifth floor, where the festivities were well underway. My colleagues and employees stood around cocktail tables, drinking champagne from tall glasses. Everyone was dressed to the nines. The men were in suits, the women in slinky cocktail dresses and the atmosphere in the room was very different from what it was on a normal workday.

"Gavin," Ernest Nolan said, coming up to me. "Happy birthday."

"Thank you, Ernie," I said with a grin, and he shook my hand. "This is Paige. Ernie is one of my investors and the life of the party."

"Oh, no," Ernest said. "The party doesn't start until Gavin arrives. It's nice to meet you."

"And you," Paige said with a smile. "This is a very lavish event for a birthday party."

"The firm insists."

"That's right. Miss Stone won't let Gavin ignore the day the way he used to. I'm glad he's got someone to celebrate it with." He looked at me. "We're having a drink at the bar a little later, right?"

"Of course."

Ernest walked away.

"Oh my God, Gavin, it's your birthday?" Paige asked, turning to me. "Why didn't you tell me?"

I shrugged. "I hate it when everything is about me."

"This whole party is about you! It's something you could have told me."

I laughed. "It's my birthday today."

Paige squeezed her eyes shut, a smile playing around her lips. "Happy birthday."

"Thank you."

"Why didn't you tell me?"

I shrugged. "They make a big deal out of it, but I hate my birthday."

"Really? Why?"

"It's a long story."

"Unhappy childhood?"

I chuckled. "Something like that."

"Don't throw me into the deep end like this. What do I say if they ask what I got you?"

"You can get creative," I said to her with a wink.

She opened her mouth to argue with me, but Melissa came up to us.

"Happy birthday, Gav," she said with a smile. "You both look incredible tonight. I made sure we have a few photographers and journalists here, and I took the liberty of inviting the tabloids personally—the invitation has your signature on it. Try to behave."

It was like a press release in disguise.

"Thanks, Mel," I said. "It's coming off well so far?"

"You bet," Melissa said. "They're all curious about Paige."

I glanced around the room, and she was right—everyone was casting curious glances in our direction.

"I guess we should go appease them, then," Paige said.

I put my hand over hers on my arm. "Let's."

The evening was charming. Everyone was perfectly agreeable. I got a ton of birthday wishes, and everyone was excited to meet Paige. She was a sweetheart. She made polite conversation with everyone and talked and laughed as if this was her world and she belonged.

Melissa came up to us after a while.

"Can I steal Paige?" she asked. "The girls are all talking, and it would be nice for you to join in."

"Oh, sure," Paige said.

"I'll be at the bar."

She nodded and leaned in to kiss me. "For show, right?" she said softly and brushed her lips against mine. I shivered and kissed her back.

"Absolutely." Her lips were soft and perfect, and she tasted like cherries. Was it her lipstick?

When she walked away with Melissa, I watched her swing her hips from side to side, mesmerized.

I shook myself and walked to the bar where Ernie and another one of my investors, Jack Berger, waited.

"Whiskey," I said to the bartender.

"And tequila," Jack added.

"Oh, no," I said. "I'm not getting shitfaced tonight."

Ernest and Jack were both a lot older than I was, but they could drink me under the table.

"Come on, you can't walk out sober on your birthday," Jack said.

"He can if he's taking a dame like Paige home tonight," Ernest said. "Have you met her?"

"I did," Jack said. "Well done, Gavin. She's an angel. Let's have a tequila on your relationship."

I laughed. I wasn't going to get out of this one.

"Okay, but I'm not having one for every birthday I've had."

"After twenty-five, that gets life-threatening, anyway," Jack said.

"Twenty-five?" I laughed. "That's a lot of tequila."

"It's a lot of years," Jack said gravely and ordered.

"Where did you find her?" Ernest asked.

"We met through mutual friends. I wasn't really looking for something, but you know how it goes."

"We do," Ernest said, exchanging a knowing look with Jack. "It's when you're not looking that Mrs. Right pops up."

Were they both happily married? I didn't even know.

"Let me tell you, she's a good one," Ernest said.

"You don't even know her," Jack said.

"I don't have to *know* her to see she's a good one. You can tell a bad apple from a mile away. Like that Tara girl you were with... I'm sorry to say it, Gavin, but she wasn't good for you."

I sighed. "Apparently, the whole world knew it, but me."

"Love is blind," Jack said.

"I'm not sure that was love."

"Well, lust can be blind, too."

I laughed. "Let's just drink, okay?"

We each took a tequila shot glass, lifted them in a toast, and threw back the alcohol. It burned down my throat, and I chased it with whiskey.

When I glanced across the room, looking for Paige, she was standing with Melissa and the investors' wives. She was talking about something, and they all hung on her every word. She looked up, our eyes locked, and she offered me a small smile.

I winked at her.

When I turned my attention back to Ernest and Jack, they both grinned at me.

"What?"

"Completely in love," Jack said.

"Infatuated."

"Whipped is what the young kids call it these days," Jack added.

I laughed. "I don't think we're far enough down the line to tell."

"You can tell right away," Ernest said. "Some people just have that something extra, and when you connect"—he snapped his fingers—"you're done."

"Aren't women supposed to be the ones who believe in soul mates and true love?" I asked with a chuckle. "You guys can give a chick flick a run for its money."

Jack snorted. "At our age, if you don't realize there's one person that brings out the best of you, you've wasted your good years. You've still to learn, Gavin. Some things in life only come by once, and if you don't take the opportunity, it won't come again."

I smiled and sipped my whiskey. I glanced at Paige again. The men didn't know what the deal was between us. Maybe they would have seen things differently if they knew. They couldn't be right about us being meant for each other.

Shit like that just didn't happen in the real world.

The night wound down, and I was only tipsy by the time we were ready to go.

Melissa came up to us to say her goodbyes.

"You did good," she said. "You're not even drunk."

I rolled my eyes. "I don't drink all the time, and it's my fucking birthday."

"It's just this year," Melissa said. "By this time next year, all of this will be behind you." Melissa turned to Paige. "You did a great job, too. They loved you. Both of you. Well done."

We left, and the valet brought my car.

"Let me drive," Paige said.

"Why?"

"You've been drinking." She glanced over her shoulder. "And I *really* want to drive the car."

I laughed and nodded. "Okay, you drive."

A thrill of excitement crossed her face, and she took the keys from the valet, who looked adequately confused.

I opened the driver's side door for her before getting in next to her. Paige started the car, and her face was a picture of pure pleasure as she pulled into the road.

"I might get a speeding ticket."

"I can afford it," I said with a laugh and sat back in the seat as Paige expertly maneuvered the car into the road and put her foot down hard.

We weaved through traffic at a speed most people would frown upon. I loved it.

"I love the way you handle the car."

"It takes skill to handle big things," she said with a sly smile.

"Oh, I know all about you handling big things."

She burst out laughing. "He says modestly."

"Hey, I know what I have to offer."

"Hmm, and you do have a *lot* to offer."

She glanced at me, and the atmosphere in the car shifted. The tension grew thick between us. I cleared my throat and turned my face to the window. I couldn't let things get like this between us.

When Paige pulled into my basement parking space, she got out of the car and handed me the keys. I stepped closer to her and studied her features. I brushed her cheek with my fingertips. Her lips were inviting, and I wanted to kiss her so fucking badly. She swallowed when I brushed my thumb along her lower lip. Her green eyes were bright, and I was aware of how close she was standing to me.

"Do you want to come up?" I asked.

"I don't think that's a good idea."

"Right." This was strictly business. I could kick myself for asking Paige to pose as my girlfriend. Ironically, it took everything off the table that we would be doing if she was my actual girlfriend.

I cleared my throat and took a step back to try to remove myself from temptation. Because fuck, I wanted her.

"Thank you for tonight," I said.

"Of course."

"I'll call you tomorrow."

She nodded. "We'll talk soon, then."

"You're okay getting home?"

"I'll book a cab. I'll be fine."

"I can have my driver take you home."

"I'll be okay, Gavin."

"Okay."

"Goodnight." She took my hand and squeezed it. When she walked away, I was acutely aware of her absence. Damn it, this was not how a night was supposed to end. On my birthday, too.

Whatever. She'd given me the biggest gift of all—after all this, Tara would leave me the fuck alone, and I could carry on with my life.

When I was sure Paige was safely on her way home, I walked to the elevator and rode my way up to the penthouse alone.

At least I would talk to her again tomorrow. As long as she was pretending to be my girlfriend, I could kiss her when we were in public.

I grinned.

I just had to make sure we were in public a lot, then.

14

Paige

The next couple of days were filled with public appearances. I went with Gavin everywhere so that we could be seen together. We went shopping—I got a couple of dresses and jewelry out of the deal—and we went for a romantic dinner date at a restaurant where a lot of celebrities ate, and paparazzi practically lived in front of the doors to see what they could find by way of fame scraps.

We went sailing on one of Gavin's yachts. Yeah, I said *one* of them because he had three.

We spent a day on the beach, sunbathing and drinking virgin cocktails—at least for me—and we swam in the ocean that was warmer than anything Seattle could ever offer.

I was starting to really like LA.

"I hate the idea of going home again," I said when we walked through the park after we'd had lunch on Sunday afternoon.

"Yeah?" Gavin licked his ice cream. We'd bought waffle cone ice creams from a stall in the park, and it was the best dessert to a nice lunch I'd ever tasted.

"Don't get me wrong, I love Seattle. I just didn't realize I would love sunshine this much. Now that I know what it can be like living in this kind of weather, I'm going to be miserable every time it rains."

"Didn't it bother you before?" Gavin asked.

I shook my head. "You don't miss what you don't know, right?"

Gavin laughed. I loved the sound of his voice. It was deep and smooth like velvet, and sometimes I just wanted to wrap myself up in the sound.

"Tell me why you hate birthdays," I said. I licked my ice cream and watched Gavin's face change as he shut himself down. I had a feeling it had to do with his past. I'd read the rumors about him being an alcoholic because his dad had been.

"There's really not that much to tell," Gavin said as he pushed one hand into his pocket. He looked around the park, not making eye contact with me. "I just hated the fact that no matter what the occasion was, my dad saw it as a reason to celebrate by drinking himself into a stupor."

"Did he hurt you?" I asked softly.

"No, he didn't."

That answer surprised me.

"He would never lay a hand on me or my mom. I should say that I'm lucky. I know violence and alcohol often go hand in hand, but my dad didn't have a temper. You see, for him to take his anger out on us would have suggested that he cared enough to go that far. He just didn't care about us at all."

I didn't say anything. I let the silence stretch thin, so Gavin could fill it if he wanted to.

He did.

"He used to tell me he was having two drinks on me because it was my birthday. There weren't any gifts, because he drank all the money. Gifts are a given with birthdays, right? I mean, it's the thought that counts, not the actual gift, and Mom always tried to make things right by baking me a cake or making special sandwiches for school that day. All the attention always ended up being on my dad at the end of the day, though, because he threw up all over the furniture or passed out naked in the front yard, and Mom and I had to get him inside, clean him up, and put him to bed."

"I'm sorry," I said. "That sounds awful."

Gavin shrugged. "It's not that part that puts me off birthdays."

"Then what?"

"I guess it's the idea of making a day all about you. I'm not the only person in this world, and it seems weird to make it all about me. I don't ever want to be like that—making everything about me when there are other people in this world, too."

"It's okay to allow yourself something, though."

"I allow myself success," Gavin said. "I allow myself what I've worked hard to earn. That's what matters. The rest..." He shrugged.

I didn't know how to answer.

"What about you?" Gavin asked.

I blinked at him. "What about me?"

"What was it like growing up?"

"Oh, nothing like how you grew up." I swallowed, feeling guilty about how simple and comfortable my life had been in comparison. "I'm the middle child of five siblings, so you can imagine how crazy it could get sometimes. Both my parents worked to support us all, and between all our hobbies and sports and drama, I don't think my mom got a lot of rest. It's only after we moved out that I think she got a chance to breathe again."

Gavin smiled. "It sounds grand."

I laughed. "It's all I knew. Ava grew up an only child, and she joined us a lot when there was trouble at home. She always said our house was like a zoo."

"Did you feel invisible?" Gavin asked.

I looked at him for a long time. How had he guessed that?

"Sometimes. Most of the time, though I don't feel invisible, I feel bland."

Gavin stopped. "If there's one thing you aren't, Paige, it's bland. You're the most interesting person I know. Hands down."

I laughed. "Thanks for that."

"I'm serious." He brushed a stray strand of hair out of my face. "You don't seem to believe what others say about you."

I shrugged. "People say a lot of things."

"They're often right." Gavin smirked. "Well, not in my case, but that's a different story. You're not all over the tabloids. Tabloids aren't right."

I giggled. "You've had a rocky road."

"Yeah. Being with Tara made my life a lot harder than it needed to be, apparently. Do you know what the worst part is?"

"What?" I asked.

"I didn't even like her that much. We were together for three years, and if I look back now, I don't even know why we were together at all. Sure, she's pretty, and we got along well enough, but there was always something missing."

"Why did you keep doing it?"

"I don't know. I didn't have a good enough reason not to."

"I get what that can be like."

"I think I need to start doing things when I have a good reason, I shouldn't *not* do them because I don't have a reason... God, that was a lot of double negatives."

I laughed.

"The good part is they're starting to cancel each other out."

"They are," Gavin said. His eyes locked on mine, and there was heat in his gaze. My breath caught in my throat. What was it about him? Every now and then, Gavin just catapulted into a different category, and he took my breath away. He had the capacity to sweep me off my feet with one stare, to make my pulse race and my knees turn to jelly.

Like now.

Gavin ran his fingers through my hair and rested his hand on my neck. His touch was warm, inviting. His eyes slid to my lips.

My stomach twisted violently, suddenly.

"Oh God," I said and stepped back. I pressed my fingers to my lips.

"What's wrong?"

"I think I'm going to—" I spun around, looking desperately for a trash can. By some miracle, I spotted one close by and ran to it. I made it just in time. My stomach ejected everything I'd just eaten as my body retched and heaved.

Gavin appeared next to me. I tried to wave him away—if there was one way I *didn't* want him to see me, it was this.

He ignored my attempt to get rid of him and scooped my hair up, holding it back for me while I threw up. If I wasn't fighting so hard to retain the last shred of dignity I had left and dying of mortification that I was vomiting my guts out in front of the hottest guy on the face of the earth, I could have melted at how sweet he was.

Finally, after what felt like forever, my body stopped revolting. I pressed the back of my hand against my mouth.

"I'm so sorry," I said. Why did they call it morning sickness if it happened at random intervals, any time of the day or night?

"Are you okay?" Gavin asked, his face riddled with concern. "Do you need to see a doctor?"

"Oh, no," I said. "I think it was... something I ate." I turned away from the trash can and squeezed my eyes shut.

"Maybe you're lactose intolerant," Gavin suggested.

I'd grown up eating ice cream.

"Maybe."

"Wait here."

He hurried away to another food stall not too far off. A moment later, he returned with a bottle of water. He handed it to me and guided me to a park bench to sit down.

"Thank you." My throat hurt when I drank the water. I drank half the bottle before I screwed the cap back on. "That wasn't very pretty to see."

"Life has ugly sides, too."

I sighed. Why was he so damn amazing? It would have been easier if he were an asshole. It would have been easier if his image had been shit because of who he was and not because of an ex who was trying to ruin his reputation. If Gavin had been a terrible person, I would have been perfectly safe.

Instead, he was so kind and caring, and the more I got to know him, the more I liked him.

I wasn't supposed to like him!

I wasn't supposed to do a lot of things, though. Like posing as his fake girlfriend. Or hide the fact that I was pregnant with his baby.

Or fall for him.

"Let's get you home so you can lie down," Gavin said.

I nodded. We stood and walked through the park. It would be better if I went home. Not because I needed the rest—morning sickness wasn't a big deal. I needed to go home so I could get away from Gavin and the butterflies that had erupted in my stomach when he was there for me. I had to get away from him so that I could think straight and talk myself down.

I wouldn't fall for him.

I wouldn't fall for him.

I wouldn't fall for him.

Except... damn it, I was.

15

Gavin

"Gavin?" Dana's voice came over the speaker on the phone.

"Yeah?"

"I have Patrick Gordon on the line for you."

"Really?"

"Can I put him through?"

When I confirmed, my phone rang, and I let it ring three times before I answered.

"Patrick, How can I help you?"

"I want to call a meeting," Gordon said.

"Oh?"

"If you're free, I'd like to do it this afternoon."

"Why?" The last I'd seen or heard of Newmark & Lewis was when they'd made a statement about me and my image in the *Finance Fortnight*.

"We have a lot to discuss."

I hesitated. I wanted to tell Gordon to go fuck himself, but that wasn't going to go down well with this new image I was working on. Melissa would have my head, for one, and it would come out, and I would look like the bad guy—again—for another.

"I can do this afternoon," I finally said. "I'm afraid I don't have a lot of time."

"Not a problem, we won't take much of your time at all."

We agreed on a time and ended the call. I stared at the phone, trying to figure out what was going on. Gordon's tone had been carefully neutral, so I had no idea what to expect. After our last meeting, I couldn't imagine what he wanted to talk about in person.

When four rolled around, I walked to the conference room where we'd had our last meeting. Dana had already set up coffee cups at the coffee station and a bowl of cookies for the men to enjoy.

I was there first. Patrick Gordon and Sean Humphrey arrived not too long after I did. Their third wheel wasn't present today.

"Please, come in. Can I get you coffee? Would you like a cookie?" I chuckled inwardly had how stupid that sounded.

"No," Gordon said. "We won't be here that long."

I nodded and pushed my hands into my pockets. Unlike the last time we'd met, I wasn't all dressed up. My sleeves were rolled up, I wasn't wearing my tie, and I wasn't in the mood to grovel. I hadn't done anything wrong, and if that was what they had in mind, coming here to pick a fight—

"We want to discuss the possibility of working together again," Gordon said, getting right down to business.

I frowned. "I thought the company name wasn't something you wanted to attach your reputation to." I didn't joke. I didn't mince my words—I was pissed off, to put it simply.

"We were wrong."

I blinked at Gordon. That was a hell of an admission.

"We might have jumped the gun a little," Humphrey said. "We were influenced by the media. We aim to please, but we're learning there's a difference between garnering respect and kissing ass."

I barked a laugh at the blunt statement, unable to stop myself. Gordon glared at Humphrey, who only shrugged.

"It's true," he said in his defense.

Gordon sighed. "Sean isn't wrong. The thing is, Core Innovations has always had a good name, and we made a mistake. We believe working together will benefit us both."

It would benefit us both, they were right, but I wasn't going to give in that easily.

"What about the article you posted about me?" I asked.

"Have you had a chance to read the paper today?" Gordon asked.

I shook my head. I'd had a full schedule, and since I'd started working on a positive image with Paige on my arm, I'd stopped looking at bad news. Melissa had insisted, and I'd agreed not to let the shit get me down but to rather focus on the good stuff.

"Here," Humphrey said, producing a tablet. He opened an internet tab, flicked the screen with his finger a few times, and turned it toward me. I stared at the screen.

"It's a public apology," Gordon said as if I couldn't read it for myself. "We retracted what we'd said before."

"This is already published?" I asked.

Gordon and Humphrey both nodded.

"We did this so you know we're serious. Even if you decide not to work together, the apology has already been released."

I frowned, shaking my head. "What changed your mind?"

"You've been doing a lot of work in public lately, and we realized that we might have seen only one side of the story."

Ah, it was because I was seen with Paige all the time, and I was behaving myself. It looked like Melissa's plan was working.

Go figure.

I thought about what they were suggesting. I'd wanted to work with them for a reason—it would boost both our businesses, and the added revenue wouldn't hurt at all. It had been a shame—and a shock—when they'd decided not to work with me.

Was I going to be a hardass and turn them down? That apology suggested they were serious, and I could still say no.

"Okay," I nodded. "Let's see where this goes."

Gordon and Humphrey both looked relieved. Maybe they'd thought I would say no. Good—I wanted them to know I wasn't going to let them trample all over me. I wanted them to be scared of me. I preferred having the leverage, and it looked like I had it. "I'll have the paperwork ready by tomorrow, and then we'll finalize the deal."

Gordon held out his hand, and we shook on it before I shook Humphrey's hand, too.

"Thank you, Gavin," Gordon said. "I think this is going to be good."

I nodded. "It has the potential to be."

When they left, I sat down in a chair nearby and let out a breath. I felt like I'd been holding it the whole time. Things were starting to look up for me. This partnership was a big one, and when I'd lost it, I'd been sure I wouldn't make it through the year.

Now, it looked like I was going to not only make it through, but there would be a substantial boost to my revenue.

That worked for me.

I left the office soon after that and drove home. On the way, I called Paige.

"What are you doing tonight?"

"I don't have any plans."

"Come over," I suggested. "I have great news."

She agreed to come over, and I ended the call. I stopped at a store and picked up ingredients for chicken parmesan—the only thing I knew how to make in my fancy kitchen—and a bottle of sparkling water because Paige seemed dead serious about not drinking, not even in private.

I was in the kitchen, slicing the chicken, when Paige arrived.

"I'm in here," I called out.

She walked into the kitchen. "What are you doing?"

"I'm cooking for us."

"Oh, that's fancy."

"It's not," I said when she came to stand next to me. "I can't cook anything else."

She giggled. "What can I help you with?"

"Would you mind cutting the vegetables?"

She shook her head, and I pointed to the brown paper bag with everything I'd bought in it. I directed her where to find a cutting board and a knife, and we worked side by side, slicing together.

"How was work?" she asked.

"Really good," I said with a smile. "We're celebrating tonight."

"Oh?"

"I had a very big business deal fall through because of all this shit with Tara, and today they came back to me, and I got it."

"Oh! Congratulations!" She wrapped her arms around my neck and planted a kiss on my cheek. My skin tingled. "Will I know what it means if you tell me what the deal is?"

"It's very technical," I admitted.

She let go of me to continue cutting, and I felt her absence.

"But it's going to do a lot for the business," I continued. "Not only revenue but future projects, too."

"That's really great."

"I invited you to celebrate with me because it wouldn't have been possible without you."

Paige blushed and smiled at me. "That's not true. You're pretty great, even without me, you know."

I chuckled. "Yeah, but you show the rest of the world. When I'm alone, I'm a dick in public and just great in private."

Paige laughed. "I'm going to agree to disagree with you."

I put the chicken in a large pan while Paige found a pot in the cupboard to put the veggies in. I liked cooking with her. It felt right to have her in my space. We were playing house together.

Sometimes, I hated that it was all an act. I could imagine us doing this for real.

When the food was in the oven, I poured us each a glass of sparkling water and added lemon and mint. We walked to the living room and lifted our glasses in a toast.

"To your success," Paige said.

"To *our* success," I corrected. "To us."

Paige giggled. "Right."

We sipped our water, and I looked at her over the rim of my glass. When she looked up at me, she blushed and averted her gaze.

We sat together in silence as the sun set and looked at the view through my large windows.

"Your view is amazing," Paige said, breaking the silence. "If I lived here, I would be here at golden hour every day."

"I don't sit here and watch the sunset very often," I admitted.

"Why not?"

"Well... I'm usually still at the office at this time. Then I go out drinking or something. Sitting here alone with my thoughts isn't the most rewarding thing after a hard day."

"Then stop thinking," Paige said.

She leaned against me, and the motion was so natural. I draped my arm over her shoulders, and she leaned in a little closer still. Her hair smelled like apple shampoo, and the warmth from her skin seeped into me, defrosting me from the inside. I felt like I'd been frozen for years. I hadn't expected it to change, but Paige awoke something in me I hadn't felt in... well, ever.

"I'm glad you're here."

Paige tilted her head, and her lips were so close to mine. "I'm glad I'm here, too."

I looked down at her, and she was a vision, a radiant goddess.

I couldn't help myself. I knew I shouldn't have done it—Paige wasn't doing this for me because she liked me or because she wanted something serious. She was doing me a favor.

Still, I couldn't stop myself. I was a moth, and Paige was the flame.

I leaned down, closed the distance between us, and kissed her.

16

Paige

When Gavin kissed me, I should have pushed him away. I should have told him this was strictly business. I was pretending to be his girlfriend, so I couldn't *actually* be his girlfriend.

I was pregnant with his child, too.

God, this was so complicated.

He slid his tongue into my mouth, and I stopped thinking. Gavin and I had been growing closer and closer the past couple of weeks, and the more I got to know him, the more I fell in love with him. He was the guy every girl wanted. He was the perfect gentleman, attentive, kind, caring. He was boyfriend material.

Hell, he was *marriage* material.

Stop thinking, I ordered myself. I was just going to drive myself crazy. Overthinking whatever this was between us wasn't going to end well for anyone.

For just a second longer, I warred with myself, trying to figure out if I should stop this.

I lost.

I didn't want Gavin to stop. I wanted him to keep going.

Gavin broke the kiss just long enough to take my water from me and put the two glasses down on the coffee table. This was a good time to tell him that this couldn't happen. It was the perfect time to—

He kissed me again.

Too late.

He nudged me so that I lay back on the couch, and he lay half on top of me. His body was large, muscular, warm. His cock was hard, grinding against me, and I moaned and trembled with need for him. I'd wanted to be with him again so badly since the first time we'd slept together. The moment I'd seen Gavin walking into his office building, I'd wanted more.

In an ideal world, I could have it all.

This just wasn't an ideal world, was it? No, it was a world where I was pretending to be something I wasn't, hiding the truth from him, and all of this was just a charade. Eventually, it would all be over, and where would that leave me?

If I wasn't careful, it would leave me with a broken heart.

Gavin cupped my breast, kneading and massaging it with a strong hand, and that was it. I stopped thinking all together.

I wrapped my arms around his neck and arched my back, pushing myself into his hand. I pushed my hands into the back of his collar and scraped my nails along the base of his neck.

He groaned into my mouth.

"You're so fucking sexy, you make me lose my mind," he muttered against my lips.

I took my cue from him and ran my nails down his back over his work shirt. He shivered and kissed me harder. The kiss became more urgent the more I ran my hands over his body. I could keep doing this all night—he was built like a god.

Gavin shifted a little, angling his body, and he tugged my shirt up. His hand landed on my bare skin, his fingers found my bra, and he pulled down the cup. He rolled my nipple between thumb and forefinger, and I gasped into his mouth. I cupped his thick cock and rubbed my hand up and down his shaft, and he groaned in response.

"Fuck, this isn't working," Gavin said, breaking the kiss and getting up.

"What?"

He took my hand and pulled me up. He tugged my top over my head, unclasped my bra, and kissed me again while he worked my jeans down my hips. I reached for his buttons and undid his shirt, fumbling until I got them all undone. I didn't push his shirt off his shoulders, I moved straight to his belt.

"Better," Gavin mumbled against my mouth when I was topless and only in my panties. "Much better."

I pulled his pants down when I got rid of his belt, and his cock sprung free. It was hard and straining, begging for the attention I was about to give it.

I sank to my knees and sucked him into my mouth. I'd wanted to do this the first time, too, but Gavin had been all over me, reducing me to a puddle of need. I wasn't much less of a creature of need now, but before he made me orgasm until I couldn't think straight anymore, I sucked his cock into my mouth.

"Fuck," Gavin bit out through gritted teeth, and he pushed his hands into my hair. He curled his hands into fists, and I bobbed my head back and forth, stroking him in and out of my mouth. His breathing came in ragged gasps as his body convulsed. I cupped his balls in one hand and massaged him, the other hand wrapped around the base of his cock where he was too large for me to take all the way.

"Paige, God, you're driving me crazy." He clenched his jaw and grunted again, and I bobbed my head faster.

Gavin pulled back, slipping out of my mouth with a plop. He grabbed my hand and pulled me up. When I stood, he kissed me hard. He tried to yank my panties off, but the flimsy material tore.

"Oh, shit."

"I didn't like them, anyway," I said and kissed him again, stepping out of the part that fell to my ankle. While I kissed him, I pulled Gavin's pants down, and he kicked them off. He got rid of the shirt he was still wearing on his arms, and then we collapsed back on the couch.

The oven timer went off, shrill and incessant.

For a moment, Gavin ignored it.

"Shit," he said when it didn't stop. "Wait here." He hurried to the kitchen, his hard cock bobbing. I sat down on the couch, breathless and aware of how naked I was. I heard Gavin taking the food out of the oven.

"Fuck!" he bit out. "Shit, fuck."

I giggled. "Are you okay?"

"This shit's hot."

He came back, shaking his hand.

"Did you burn yourself?" I asked.

"Not too badly," he said and studied his finger.

"Let me see." I took his hand. His finger wasn't red or anything—it wasn't serious at all. I pressed my lips against his fingertip before I sucked his finger into my mouth. I looked him in the eye while I swirled my tongue around his finger, sucking it as I would suck his cock. He stared at me, lips parted.

"Fuck, Paige." He growled and yanked back his hand. He grabbed me and kissed me, and we fell backward onto the couch again.

When he climbed onto me, my legs fell open for him. I was ready for him, but Gavin paused.

"Just hang on." He got up and found his wallet on the table by the door, and retrieved a condom.

My stomach twisted—a condom was pointless now. I was already pregnant, but he didn't know that. I watched him roll it over his cock before he climbed onto me again. His cock knew where to go, and when he pushed into me, I moaned. He pounded into me, his hips bucking against mine. He fucked me hard and fast right away, taking me with an intensity that matched my need for him.

I cried out loudly, my sounds in rhythm with his thrusts.

It didn't take long before an orgasm rocked my body. I moaned and held onto Gavin's shoulders, gasping as the pleasure took my breath away. He slowed his pace, sensually stroking in and out of me while I orgasmed, dragging it out. I gasped for breath, and my body contracted around him, clamping down on his cock.

Gavin groaned.

When the orgasm faded, I lay on the couch, trembling. Gavin was still inside me, but he lay still and planted kisses on my face. The display of affection washed warmth through me. This wasn't just sex. It didn't *feel* like just sex. It felt like two people, in love, connecting with each other.

It wasn't true. I had to remind myself this was just like the first time. This was just sex, and afterward, we would go back to being good friends.

Gavin and I were close, but this...

"Stop thinking," he told me.

"How do you know I'm thinking?"

"I can see it," he said and kissed me. "Don't."

His tongue slid into my mouth again, and we made out while he was buried inside me. I let him kiss me until I couldn't stand it anymore.

"Keep going, Gavin," I urged.

He grinned at me. "Do you want me to?"

I groaned, frustrated. "Why don't you just sit back."

Gavin did as I asked and shifted so that he sat on the couch. I wanted to be on top of him. I wanted to finish him off the way he'd done for me.

I straddled his lap, wrapped my fingers around his slick cock and guided it to my entrance. We both moaned when I sank down on him, and Gavin's eyes filled with lust. He clenched his jaw and sucked his breath through gritted teeth. He moved his hands to my hips, and when I started rocking back and forth, his fingers dug into my skin.

I moaned, feeling tighter after my orgasm, and Gavin felt amazing inside me. I was raw after our sex so far, and every movement pulsed through me like an electric shock. I pushed down hard so that he drove deep into me and rocked my hips, stroking myself on his cock. My clit rubbed against his pubic bone, and I locked my eyes on him while I rocked harder and faster.

Gavin's face was pure pleasure. His lips were parted, and his eyes rolled back in his head as he panted and moaned. He used his hands on my hips to rock me back further and pull me forward harder, and another orgasm was building inside me. His cock stroked my G-spot, and his hands, gripping my hips, added a delicious burst of pain that translated into pure pleasure, and I was on the edge of another orgasm.

Gavin was on the edge, too. He grew even bigger inside me, and his breathing became shallow and erratic. He moaned louder as I rocked back and forth, and I rode him to his orgasm and mine. His hands on my hips kept up the rhythm.

When I orgasmed, my body tightened, and I cried out. I fell forward against him, and Gavin put his hand on my chin and kissed me. He swallowed my cries and bucked his hips, helping me ride out the orgasm. It pushed him over the edge, and he cried out into my mouth. He thrust into me as far as he could go, and his hand on my hip dug into my skin as he climaxed. I felt his muscles contract against me, his cock jerked and throbbed inside me, and he stopped breathing for a moment, his face contorted in a mask of pure ecstasy.

It felt like it carried on forever, but eventually, the waves of pleasure started to fade, and Gavin and I were tangled together in the aftermath. I gasped, and he held onto me, his heart hammering against my chest.

I clambered off him, my body numb, legs like jelly. I collapsed on the couch, and Gavin lay down with me. Our skin was slick with sweat, and we were still breathing hard.

"The food smells amazing," I said in a breathy voice.

"Hmm," Gavin said. "I'm ravenous now."

"Me too," I said with a giggle.

Gavin lifted his head and planted a kiss on my lips.

"Come on, let's eat."

"Let's celebrate."

He grinned at me. "I think we already did that."

I blushed, but Gavin got up and helped me find my clothes, and nothing with him was ever awkward or uncomfortable.

Damn it, why did every single thing about him have to be so lovable?

If he didn't start doing something that turned me off and made me dislike him soon, I was going to be in *big* trouble.

17

Gavin

"Morning," I said brightly to Melissa when I found her in my office.

"You're in a good mood," she said. Her blonde hair was back in a bun, and she wore her usual dress suit. The only thing that changed about Melissa was the color of her dress suit or whether her hair was up or down. She had no idea how much I appreciated her consistency in a world where everything felt like it could spin out of control at any moment.

I dropped into my leather chair. I flipped my laptop open and powered it up.

"I have reason to be, right? I mean, things are going really well. I got Newmark & Lewis, everyone that meets Paige loves her, and it looks like Tara is actually hanging back. I never thought I'd see the day."

"Things are going really well," Melissa agreed. "You have a better reputation, and you haven't been in the tabloids in a while."

I grinned. "No news is good news, right?"

"If they leave you alone, it's definitely good news."

I stretched in my chair until my back popped. "It looks like I'm finally free of Tara. I wouldn't have thought of having a fake girlfriend myself—Paige is a genius."

"So, you're still on the fake girlfriend channel, huh?" Melissa asked.

I blinked at her. "What do you mean?"

Melissa shrugged. "When the two of you are together, it doesn't look fake at all."

"It's so that everyone believes it's real," I pointed out. "It would be a shitshow if it came out it's not real."

Melissa shook her head. "That's not what I'm trying to say."

"Then what?"

She leaned back in her chair and studied me, looking like she was trying to decide how to word it.

"Do you like her?"

"Of course I like her."

Melissa rolled her eyes. "Don't play dumb with me, Gavin. You know what I'm asking you."

I sighed. "I know. I like her, yeah. We're good together. *Really* good. It scares me how well she fits into my life."

"So? Why don't you make it official? It will do your image good, but that's been taken care of. It will do your heart good, too. You deserve someone who makes you happy, and when you're with her, you light up like a Christmas tree."

I shook my head. "It's not real, Mel. We're playing pretend. She doesn't want a relationship. She's doing me a favor, and I'm not going to put pressure on her for anything else than she's already doing for me."

"Can't you talk to her?"

"There's nothing to talk about. I'm keeping her away from her life in Seattle longer than she should be gone as it is. Besides, what do I have to offer her? A shitty past? She doesn't deserve this hell with my dad, no matter which way you look at it."

"Don't you think that's for her to decide?"

I shook my head. "I get the whole personal choice thing, but I don't want to do that to her, and that should be enough of a reason not to drag her under. Besides, my life is so volatile, and she has a stable life in Seattle. She deserves that."

Melissa pursed her lips. She didn't agree with me, but she didn't get it. Paige wasn't like any other woman I'd ever been with. I hadn't cared about my shitty past and the way the press kept bringing it up when it was convenient when Tara was in my life because Tara didn't care about the drama. In fact, she begged for it, and I didn't feel like she needed to be sheltered.

With Paige, it was different. Everything about her was beautiful and interesting and perfect. Fuck saying she didn't deserve the bullshit with my dad, *I* didn't deserve her. She deserved Prince Charming, and I was just a shitty frog.

"If you love her, Gavin, you should shoot your shot."

"I didn't say anything about love," I pointed out.

"No, but I've known you for nearly a decade, and I'm not stupid," Melissa said.

"You're also not scared to speak your mind," I grumbled.

Melissa grinned at me and packed up her things. "Yeah, that's what you pay me for."

She was right.

"What did you need to see me about?" I asked when Melissa got ready to leave. "Weren't you here for a reason?"

"I just wanted to tell you things are going according to plan and to make sure you're happy. It's all good, Gavin. You're almost in the clear."

I nodded. "It's good to know this nightmare with Tara is behind me."

"We'll talk soon, Gavin," Melissa said with a smile. "Think about what I said."

She left my office, and I leaned back in my chair and sighed. It was easy for Melissa to say, "If you love her, make it happen," but it wasn't so easy to execute. I was already asking so much of Paige, and she gave it without hesitation. I wasn't going to put even more pressure on her, no matter how I felt about her. We had an understanding, and it worked for us right now.

The thing was, Paige and I had become very close friends. I could share my life with her. I could talk to her about anything. When something big happened, when I woke up with a weird dream, when I thought about something stupid—anything silly or crazy or huge—I wanted to tell her about it. Not Parker, not Noah.

Paige.

What if I told her I loved her, and she told me she didn't feel the same? Hell, she was bound to say that. Yeah, we slept together, but that didn't mean love was involved. I'd slept with Tara for three years, and I'd realized I never really loved her.

I didn't want to lose Paige as a friend. Besides, being the guy who fell in love with her because we were pretending somehow sounded pathetic.

I was Gavin fucking Austin. I didn't sound pathetic. I had Melissa around to ensure that.

No, telling Paige I was in love with her would be a mistake on so many levels. We just had to ride out this thing we were stuck in now, and then when it was all over, maybe I could think straight again.

My phone rang.

"Yeah?" I asked, picking up Dana's line.

"You have a Mr. Austin on line two."

I stilled. What the fuck was my dad doing calling me on the work line? What the fuck was he doing calling me at all?

"I'm not taking it."

"Are you sure?"

"I'm busy."

"Okay."

I put the phone down. My good mood had drained away, and a black mood crept in.

The phone rang again.

"He's asking when a good time would be to call you back."

"Never. You can quote me on that."

"Gavin…"

I put the phone down. I was getting pissed off.

My dad hadn't bothered to reach out to me in years. He'd tried once or twice after I'd left, when I'd started showing up in the papers, when I'd made my millions, but I didn't want to hear what he had to say. Nothing I'd achieved in life had been thanks to him or his input. He probably just wanted money, anyway.

Money he could drink away—that was the only thing he knew how to do.

I wouldn't talk to him. Hell, it would be a mistake to talk to him now, anyway. All eyes were on me, and in the wake of what Tara had said about me and alcohol, associating with my dad at all would bring this carefully constructed house of cards Paige and I had built crashing down again.

My dad could fuck off once and for all. I wished he would.

The rest of the day wasn't as good as it could have been. I'd been in a great mood when I'd arrived at the office, but after my dad's call, I was pissed off and grumpy. To make matters worse, I had to deal with clients who were full of shit, one of my cargo ships got lost in a storm, and the families were panicked about the missing crew, and Tara tried to call me, too.

She'd tried to call my personal number—even when I'd told her to make an appointment with Dana so that my secretary could shun her instead of me doing it again—and I'd had to decline the call twice before turning the stupid piece of shit off completely.

By the time I drove home, my mood was blacker than black.

When I arrived at the apartment, the lights were on, and the smell of home-cooked food tugged at me when I walked in.

Paige came from the kitchen.

"Oh, hi," I said, surprised to see her. "What are you doing here?"

"I'm making supper," she said. "I thought you could use a home-cooked meal for a change rather than the restaurant food you keep ordering up."

I took a deep breath and groaned. "It smells amazing. Come here."

I snaked my arm around her waist and pulled her tightly against me. I hugged her and poured all my frustration out, letting her warmth push it away.

"Are you okay?" she asked when I finally let go of her. Her eyes scanned my face.

"I had a rough day at the office, that's all." She had no idea what a treat it was to come home to her after a long day.

"I'm sorry. Here." She walked to the kitchen and came back with an ice-cold beer. "I thought it could help take the edge off."

"Where have you been all my life?" I asked with a grin.

Paige laughed. "Sit with me while I cook. Tell me about your crap day. I'll tell you about mine, and we can trade."

"You had a crap day?"

Paige nodded and walked to the stove, where she mixed a red marinara in a saucepan. She lifted the wooden spoon and held it out to me.

I blew on the sauce before I tasted it.

"Oh my God." I groaned. "Are you fucking kidding me?"

"What?" she asked.

"You're a whiz in the kitchen. How didn't I know about this?"

She laughed. "My mom made us all do cooking turns while we were in the house. With five kids, it gets a lot, so we had to team up, and we took turns through the week. When you have to cook for as many people as we were, and as often as we had to, you learn a thing or two."

I shook my head, picked up my beer, and walked to the breakfast nook. I watched Paige as she walked around my kitchen, more and more at home. She knew where everything was by now—pots and pans, cups and glasses, plates...

"So, tell me about your day."

Paige sighed. "I think I'm getting on Ava's nerves. She's cranky these days, and Warner is under the weather. The combo is tough. I'm trying to stay out of her way mostly, but—"

"Why is she cranky?" I asked. "She's never cranky. Ava has to be the brightest, most positive person I know."

"Yeah." She glanced at me. "Can you keep a secret?"

"Of course."

Paige laughed. "I don't know if I trust you..."

"Hey, I kept our secret, right?"

She giggled. "Okay, I guess so... They're not announcing it for another couple of weeks, but Ava's pregnant."

My eyes widened. "Oh, wow."

"Yeah. I think her hormones are crazy, and then dealing with Warner *and* a houseguest gets a bit much."

"I don't envy her."

Paige frowned. "Why?"

"Having to give up so much of your time and who you are as a person to kids? That doesn't sound like my idea of fun."

Paige stilled. "You don't ever want to have kids?"

I snorted. "I would have to have a woman in my life for that, first. Even then, I don't know if I would ever go there. I had a shitty run with my dad. This world is a fucked up place if what happened with Tara is any indication... why would I want to bring a kid into this world?"

"It doesn't have to be that way, you know," Paige said softly.

I shrugged. "Why take the risk? There's more to life than kids."

"Hmm," Paige said. She put pasta in a pot, added salt, and put the pot on the stove to bring the water to a boil.

"Move in with me," I blurted out.

Paige snapped her head to me. "What?"

"Just for a few days. You know, to get out of Ava's hair for a bit. Unless..." What if she didn't want it? "You can stay in a spare bedroom, you don't need to stay in my room or anything." She still looked flustered. Shit. "If you want to stay in a hotel instead, I'll pay for it."

The longer Paige stayed quiet, the more I panicked I'd said something stupid. What the fuck had I been thinking?

The truth was, I hadn't thought at all. I just wanted her here with me, someone caring and warm to come home to, like tonight. It had never been like this with previous women who'd lived with me. With Paige in my house, coming home really felt like coming *home*.

"Tell me about *your* day," Paige said softly.

I groaned. "Are you sure you want to hear about what a shitshow it's been?"

Paige grinned. "Hit me, Austin. I can handle it."

I laughed and told her about everything that had gone wrong, from tough clients to lost cargo ships and scared families. Paige was supportive. She was a good listener, and it was so easy to talk to her.

"I'm sure tomorrow will be better," Paige said when she pulled the cooked pasta off the stove. She took two bowls out of the cabinet and dished up pasta for each of us. She added the marinara sauce and fried bacon bits.

We walked to the dining room table.

"This is incredible," I said, taking a bite. It was simple, and it was delicious. "You should teach me how to make this sauce."

"It's an old family recipe," Paige said with a grin. "My gran will lose her shit if she knows I'm giving it out to random people."

"I'm not random people," I pointed out.

Paige laughed and shook her head. "Sorry, can't go against family, right?"

My heart sank, and my smile faded. Paige's family sounded so amazing. I couldn't imagine what it had to be like to have so many people in your corner, not because they had to be, but because they wanted to be. Because they were all related. I'd never had anything like that. I hadn't known my grandparents on either side of the family, and I'd barely had parents.

"My dad tried to call me today," I said quietly. I scraped the pasta around in my bowl, not making eye contact with Paige.

"What did he say?"

I shook my head. "I didn't take the call. I don't want to talk to him."

I'd told Paige about my dad and my past with him. Not everything, but the important parts—he'd chosen alcohol over us, and I'd left him behind to build a better life.

"Why not?" she asked carefully.

"He probably just wants money."

"Is that what he wanted before?"

I shrugged. "I don't know. I didn't bother to find out what he wanted then, either. I just sent the money to him and got it over with."

Paige didn't answer, and when I glanced at her, her eyes were on her food, too.

"Maybe you should find out what he wants," she finally said. "What if he doesn't want money? What if he wants to make things right?"

"What's there to make right?" I asked with a snort. "It's too late to change what happened. My childhood is long gone. He can't do anything about that now."

Paige studied me. I felt her eyes on my face. When I glanced up at her, her green eyes were gentle.

"Maybe he wants to tell you he's sorry."

"And then I'll have to forgive him," I pointed out. "That just means I'll owe him something *again*. It always ends up with me having to give him something."

Paige reached over the table and put her hand on mine. Her touch was warm.

"You've never owed him anything. He owes you something. Give him the chance to give it to you, if he wants. You might feel better afterward."

I shook my head. I didn't know if I would. It just wasn't that simple.

"Think about it," Paige said. "Just remember, at the end of it all, it's up to you. You're in control here."

I hadn't thought about it that way. It *was* my decision. I was in control. I hadn't felt like I was in control in a long time.

Maybe ever.

Fuck if I would admit that, though.

"Thank you," I said to Paige.

"For what?"

"Listening."

Paige smiled. "Of course. I'm always here, Gavin. We may have an act out to the world that we're together, but behind closed doors, we're still us."

I nodded and returned her smile. I loved the way she'd said that. If she only knew how much.

"Okay," she said.

"What?"

"I'll stay here for a couple of days."

My grin broadened.

"Yeah?"

She giggled. "Yeah, why not? I mean, what's the worst that could happen?"

The worst was that I could fall even more for her than I already had, but it was just my heart on the line here.

I was willing to take that risk. Maybe I would regret it later, but right now, it was what I wanted.

18

Paige

"You really don't have to do this," Ava said, coming into my room as I packed my things. "I don't want you to go."

"I know you guys need your space, Av," I said. "I've been in your hair long enough. It's just a couple of days."

Ava sighed and sank onto my bed. She lay back against the pillows and put her hand on her lower stomach.

"How are you feeling?"

"You would think I'm eight months in with how tired I am. My back is killing me, and I can't keep anything down. I was *so* excited when I found out I was pregnant again. Now, I just want it over."

"It gets better after a while, doesn't it?"

Ava narrowed her eyes at me. "It's supposed to, although you seem perfectly fine."

"I'm not as far along as you are," I pointed out.

"Yeah, and you're handling it like a pro."

"Maybe physically..."

"You're not okay emotionally?"

I shrugged and folded a top, putting it into my bag. "I don't know how I feel yet. I keep thinking I have to figure it out, but I just never get there."

"It's a big thing to have a baby, especially in your situation," Ava said. "Don't be too hard on yourself. I know how tough it can be."

Ava had gotten pregnant accidentally too, when she and Noah had faked a marriage to fool his dad. It had been a messy story, and it was ridiculous how similar our situations were now.

"At least you were already married," I said with a grin.

Ava rolled her eyes. "What's with us and making terrible choices?"

"Best friends—we do it all together."

Ava laughed.

"So, how is this going to work?" she asked.

"What?"

"Your living with him."

"I'm moving into a spare room, and I'll be there for a couple of days before I come back. I think it's all going to be over soon. His PR manager is super happy with how things are going, so we don't have to keep doing this forever."

Ava hesitated. "Do you *want* to do this forever?"

I shook my head. "It won't work."

"That's not what I asked."

I sighed. "I know it won't work, so whether I want it or not is irrelevant."

"What makes you think it won't work?"

I looked at Ava. "I'm pregnant."

"Yeah? It's his baby. I mean, sometime you're going to have to face this and actually figure it out with him. I can't believe you haven't told him yet."

I folded a pair of jeans and packed them.

"It's not that simple." When Ava stayed silent, inviting me to fill the silence, I did. "He doesn't want kids."

"What?" Ava asked, shocked. "How do you know?"

"He told me," I said with a nonchalant shrug. Inside, I was reeling. When I'd heard that Gavin didn't want kids, I'd died on the inside.

"When did you even talk about this? Without you telling him you're having a baby, that doesn't make any sense."

"Actually…" I glanced at Ava, suddenly remembering how we'd gotten on the topic, and a pang of guilt shot into my chest. "I might have told him that you're pregnant."

"What!" Ava cried out. "You told him *I'm* pregnant and not you?"

"Well it sounds really messed up when you say it like that," I muttered. I couldn't tell her the whole thing and make her feel even worse about me leaving. I'd told Gavin she was pregnant to justify how cranky she was. None of it would come out right.

God, it was already so twisted.

"Yeah, it does," Ava said tightly. "I wanted to announce it and everything."

"I know, I'm sorry! I don't know what I was thinking. He won't tell anyone though."

Ava pursed her lips. "Tell me why he doesn't want to have kids."

I sighed. "He said he doesn't see why he should bring a child into this world when it's all fucked up. He doesn't have a great relationship with his dad."

"Yeah, I've heard that on the news more than once."

I nodded. "I guess if everyone keeps rubbing it in his face, it doesn't really let him forget about it, either."

"He might feel different about it when he realizes he actually has a baby coming," Ava pointed out. "In theory, it's easy to make assumptions about how you would feel or react, but when it really happens, it's a different story."

I shook my head. "It doesn't matter. I'm not going to tell him."

"Why not? He deserves to—"

"Yeah, I know, but I won't put him or myself through that." I zipped my bag shut. "If I know he's going to tell me he doesn't want any part of it, I can spare myself the heartache and him the embarrassment of saying something that I know he'll feel bad about, too."

Ava looked at me, incredulous. "You're just going to have the baby alone, then?"

"I won't be alone. I'll have my family. There are already so many babies, what's one more?"

"You haven't told your family, either."

"Eventually, someone will notice," I said with a grin, trying to make light of the situation. It wasn't funny, though. Ava didn't laugh, and my smile faded.

"Just think about it, okay?" Ava said. "You don't have to have him in your life, but you can't keep it a secret from him. You're going to need someone on your side."

I nodded. "I'll think about it." That was the least I could do, right? I could still decide I wasn't going to tell him, go back to Seattle, and raise the baby alone.

Ava walked with me to the front door.

"You know you don't have to go."

"I'm not going forever," I said and hugged her. "I'm just around the corner, anyway. We can have lunch or go shopping every day if you want to."

Ava laughed. "You might as well stay, then."

I smiled at my best friend before I left, walking to the gate where a cab was going to pick me up to take me to Gavin's place. Ava watched me get into the car and go.

It was easy for her to say I had to tell Gavin. She'd already been through it all; she knew what her happy ending looked like. I didn't know what mine would be yet. There were still too many questions, and it wasn't so easy just to close my eyes and jump.

One thing I did know—Gavin had been through his fair share of hell, and he didn't need me to add to that. Especially when the question I would ask was one I already had an answer to.

No, it was better this way. I would have my fun, Gavin and I would be what we were, and when it was all over, I would go back to Seattle and start a new chapter in my life.

Alone.

I'd said I wanted an adventure, right?

It just didn't look exactly as I'd hoped it would.

19

Gavin

Having Paige live with me was even better than I'd thought it would be. Coming home to her after work was a treat. She was just absolutley perfect in every way.

All I needed was for us to be together for real and not leave our relationship outside my door every time we came back after a night out together.

I pushed that idea out of my mind as far as I could. She was staying in a different room, she was doing me a favor, but this wasn't her life.

"I think you're being an idiot," Parker said. He lifted the barbell and blew out his breath so that his cheeks billowed before pulling a god-awful face when he lowered the bar to his chest again.

"Why?" I asked. I was standing behind him, spotting him so that I could grab the bar and help him out if something went wrong. Judging by the way his arms trembled and the contorted look on his face, he was going to need me pretty soon.

"I think it's downright dumb," Ryan chimed from where he was doing free-weight bicep curls not too far off. He sat on a bench and studied his bulging muscles with every curl.

"How about you stop teaming up on me and actually tell me what the fuck you mean."

Parker held the bar up, his elbows nearly locked, and glanced at Ryan. I hated how close they were sometimes, with their unspoken conversations and inside jokes. I loved both of them, they were great friends, but it was clear sometimes that I'd come into the picture much later.

"You're snappy," Ryan said.

"Yeah, because Mr. Trembles over here isn't finishing up, and I'm getting cold just standing here spotting him."

Parker lowered the bar again and lifted it. He put it on the stand and rolled out from underneath it.

"Okay, okay, don't get your panties in a twist," he said with a laugh.

I got onto the bench and lifted the bar. I hadn't bothered taking some of Parker's weights off. As soon as I lifted the bar off the stand, I regretted it. We worked in pyramids with the weights, starting a little lower and pushing up the weights with each set.

Fuck if I was going to admit this was too much. I lowered the bar, and my face turned red as I pushed it back up again.

"Are you going to tell me or what?" I asked, lowering the bar again. I didn't dare look at Parker. No doubt, his eyes would be filled with laughter at my struggle to get the weight up on my first set.

"You should just tell her how you feel," Ryan said from the side.

"Yeah," Parker agreed. "I know you said you're just friends, and you're always on about the shit that you don't deserve better, blah, blah, fucking blah. Just tell her."

"Yeah, you never know. Maybe she feels the same, and then you're cutting yourself off at the knees for nothing," Ryan said.

"What if she says she *doesn't* feel the same?" I countered.

That was the real problem, wasn't it? If she didn't feel the same way I felt about her, then I would look like an idiot.

"It's not wrong to risk it," Parker said. "And if she turns you down, then good riddance, she doesn't know how great you are, and then you *really* don't deserve her, *you* deserve better."

I lifted the bar onto the stand. I couldn't complete my set because it was too fucking heavy, and that pissed me off even more.

"How am I supposed to do it?"

Parker walked around the bench to look me in the eye. I sat up, breathing hard.

"You just tell her. Something like this: 'Paige, I'm in love with you.' "

I snorted. "You're a real poet."

"Hey, they don't keep me around for this face," Parker said and formed an L with his thumb and forefinger, pressing it against his chin. "I'm actually smart, too."

Ryan snorted. "They're just too scared to lose your cash and tell you you're not all that smart."

Parker rolled his eyes before he looked at me. He was grinning, though—he and Ryan always gave each other shit. It was their love language or something.

"Just do it, man. You dated Tara. You survived a huge storm of pure shit because of her. You can do this."

"Hmm."

"You know what I think your real issue is?" Ryan asked, putting down his weights. He shook his hands, mopped his face with a towel, and grabbed his water bottle.

"What?" I asked while he sucked on the bottle, making a dent in it as he drank so much before coming up for air.

"I think you didn't care about Tara that much, so what she did after you broke up was just annoying, not painful. You care enough about Paige that it will hurt if she decides to turn her back on you."

I pulled a face. "And you know this for a fact?" I was trying to be macho about it, but Ryan was fucking right.

Parker and Ryan glanced at each other again. I groaned and fell back on the bench. Maybe they had a point. Maybe telling Paige wouldn't be the worst thing in the world. No, *losing* her would be the worst thing, but I'd been through hell and back, and I could figure it out, right? She was going back to Seattle soon, so if it didn't work out, I wouldn't have to see her or run into her and be reminded of it.

Maybe it was worth a shot.

"I'm out, guys."

"You didn't even finish your workout," Parker said.

"Yeah, I have shit to do." I walked away from them.

"You're going to tell her?" Ryan called after me.

"I don't know."

"That's a yes," Parker exclaimed, and their laughter and cheers followed me all the way into the men's locker room.

I didn't want this to become a big thing. I didn't want to make a fuss and put myself and Paige on the spot so that it became awkward. I didn't want to tell her while we were making coffee, either.

Finally, I decided to do it on one of my yachts. I chose the smallest one. The Scout 530 LXF was my favorite, a Scout boat with all the luxuries and entertainment features that made it a pleasure to be in. I made a couple of calls, took care of a few things, and finally, I drove back to the apartment to find Paige.

She was lying on the couch watching a home makeover show when I came in.

"Hi," she said, sitting up. She wore black sweatpants and a white tank top, and she was so fucking sexy.

"I was thinking… we should do pizza tonight."

"Pizza?" I asked, snapping out of my daze.

"Yeah, don't you ever get pizza from your fancy restaurants?"

I chuckled. "My fancy restaurants don't serve pizza."

"I love pizza," she said with a small pout.

"Okay, we'll get pizza…" Her eyes lit up. "But not tonight."

She frowned.

"I have a surprise for you."

"What?"

"I want to take you out."

"Why?"

Why did she have so many questions? It was hard to surprise her if she was going to be like this.

"Because you've been through a lot with me, and I want to show you how much I appreciate you." That wasn't a lie. I appreciated her more than she would ever know.

"Okay… what should I wear?"

"Something nice but comfortable. I'm wearing khakis and a button-up shirt."

"Okay."

I smiled, watching her hips swing side to side when she walked to the spare room to get dressed before I walked to the main bedroom to do the same.

When I came out of the room a half an hour later, Paige was ready. She wore black leggings with a flowing green top that made her eyes look like jewels. Her hair was fashioned in a messy kind of bun at her neck, and she wore black flats.

"You look great," I said with a smile.

She blushed lightly, and I walked to the door and held it for her.

My stomach twisted in knots while we drove to the marina. I tried all the different ways I could tell her how I felt.

You've become really special to me.

You're my best friend.

You're damn good in bed.

I grinned at the last statement.

I'm in love with you.

"What do you think the chances are the paparazzi will follow us?" Paige asked, pulling me out of my thoughts.

"I think it will be fine. There's not usually much to see in the marina at night."

"We're going to the marina?"

I nodded and headed toward the waterside. I parked my car and opened the car door for Paige. She smiled.

"We haven't done something on the water at night before," Paige said. I'd had her on my bigger yachts for two separate work functions.

"Yeah, this will be nothing like before. At night, there's a different kind of magic out there."

"It sounds like a movie," Paige said with a giggle.

I hoped the movie would have a happy ending.

Marina Del Rey was huge, with five-thousand boats at anchor. It was peaceful at night. A few people partied on their yachts, but the sound was muted, and only the laughter skipped across the water.

We arrived where my Scout lay in the water, bobbing gently.

"Oh, I love it," Paige said when she saw the boat. She had an affinity for powerful engines. It was so hot that she liked things like that. We climbed on board, and I stepped behind the wheel. She sat down in the passenger seat, and I started the engine, taking us out of the marina and into the open ocean.

When we were some distance away from the shore, I cut the engine, and we bobbed gently on the swell.

The LA coastline was beautiful with all the twinkling lights. Above us, the stars were bright—a diamond bowl upended—and there wasn't a cloud in the sky.

"You were right," Paige said. "This is a different kind of magic."

I smiled at her and held out my hand. She took it, and I led her to the back of the boat where I'd set up a table. Now that we weren't moving, I took out everything I'd had in cubbies—a white tablecloth, roses, small lights that were in lieu of candles, and a picnic basket I'd had a friend at a five-star restaurant prepare for me.

"This is probably the most private place we can be," Paige mused. "The paparazzi won't find us here at all."

"That's what I was hoping for," I said and opened a bottle of sparkling water. "Just you and me and no reason to put on a face. Tonight, we're just us."

Paige smiled at me. "I like us."

I was counting on that. I wanted "us" to be more than just close friends who shared a secret.

I wanted to make "us" official.

20

Paige

Everything about tonight was perfect. Gavin was the ideal gentleman, and he'd made such an effort to get us to a place where we didn't have to worry about what we did around each other and how we acted.

It had been a tough road to pretend to be together. It had been even harder since it was what I would have wanted.

"This is really good," I said, biting into roasted lamb that was so tender it fell from the bone.

"It is," Gavin agreed.

My stomach rolled, and I paused. If I threw up now, it would ruin the whole night.

"Are you okay?" Gavin asked. He picked up on my moods so quickly—he was attentive as hell. Usually it was a great trait in a guy. Tonight, I wished he wasn't so tuned into what I felt and how I reacted. I wanted him to just be a regular guy who missed most of what was going on.

"I just feel a little off," I said carefully.

"It's the rocking," Gavin said, nodding. "The smaller yachts bob on the waves so much more than the large ones, and it's easier to get seasick."

"Right," I said. "That must be it. I'm sure it will pass as soon as I get used to it."

Gavin nodded.

"What are your plans after this?" I asked.

"After what?"

"After all this passes and you can live your life again," I said. "You must be excited to be able to just move on and do your own thing again."

"Yeah, it will be nice to leave all this behind."

I nodded and stared at the wild rice that came with the lamb.

"I don't want to pretend anymore," Gavin said.

"Well, soon you won't have to." Was he that eager for this to be over?

"It was harder than I thought it would be."

Was it really? I'd thought being with Gavin had been easy, comfortable, warm. I'd hoped he felt the same. I hadn't realized it had been so hard on him.

"As soon as Melissa gives the word, we can stage some kind of public breakup, and then I'm on the first plane home."

Gavin frowned. "Is that what you want? To go home?"

"I've been living out of a suitcase for weeks. It will be nice to be able to unpack and breathe again."

"Right," Gavin said. "Seattle is calling." He looked irritated. He speared a piece of lamb, but instead of taking a bite, he put his knife and fork down with a clatter and got up. "I need something stronger than water. You don't want something better than... that?"

I shook my head, and he walked around the boat, opening a cooler. He produced a bottle of whiskey and poured himself a glass.

"You don't have to keep up the act, you know."

"What act?" I asked, confused.

"The no-drinking thing you're doing so you're a saint to the public. Your efforts paid off, it worked, but we're alone now."

"I'm not trying to put up an act," I defended. Should I just tell him I was pregnant and get it over with? He didn't look like he was in the right frame of mind to receive information like that. Maybe a moment ago, but now he was angry for some reason.

Gavin snorted in response to my statement.

"Why are you upset?" I asked.

"I'm not upset."

I raised my eyebrows. He'd suddenly decided he needed a drink, and he was irritated about a conversation he'd initiated. None of it made sense.

Gavin shook his head. "It's nothing. I was an idiot, buying into the picture we painted for the rest of the world."

"What are you talking about?" I asked with narrowed eyes. "You're making it sound like I somehow misled you."

"Didn't you?"

I scoffed, shocked at where this conversation was going.

"I can't believe this," I said and sat back. I felt sick again, but not because of my pregnancy. This time, it was my emotions playing up. Gavin was being weird. He was upset about something, slinging around accusations, and this was not like him. "Maybe we should go back to the shore after all."

"Let's just cut the whole thing short, then," Gavin said. "Not just the date, but all of it."

I gasped. "What the hell has gotten into you?"

Gavin shook his head and threw back his alcohol in one big gulp. He refused to look at me, so I got up and marched the short distance across the deck to him.

"Don't you dare blame me for this," Gavin said. "It's not like I did it on purpose."

"Did what?" I asked. "I don't know what you're trying to—"

"I'm in love with you!" he blurted out.

I blinked at him.

"There, I said it. I'm fucking in love with you, and the idea of you leaving again pisses me off. I'd hoped you felt the same, but if you want to go, you should just go. There's no point dragging this out any longer. I just... I had to say that to you."

I stared at Gavin. His little outburst, his inability to have a straight-forward conversation, was because he didn't know how to put what he felt into words.

It had to be the dumbest and the sweetest thing I'd ever seen.

"Gavin..." He looked at me with a resigned expression. "I'm in love with you, too."

His face changed from resignation to surprise to something I couldn't catch before he grabbed me and kissed me.

I kissed him back. His tongue slid into my mouth, and he wrapped his arms around my waist, pulling me tightly against him. I moaned into his mouth. I'd wanted to kiss him so many times. I'd wanted to tell him how I felt so many times, but I'd been too scared he didn't feel the same.

Had he struggled with the same battle all this time?

A small voice at the back of my mind screamed at me.

Tell him you're pregnant.

I couldn't. If I told him now, it would ruin everything. It was selfish of me, but I wanted him. I wanted him to be in love with me for a while before he turned his back on me and the baby. Inevitably all this was going to end, so I would take as much of it as I could get while I could get it.

Just for a short time, I wanted to love and be loved in return.

Gavin kissed me like he wanted to devour me. He grinded himself against me, and he was already hard. Lust washed over me and pooled between my legs, and the sexual tension between us was thick.

I wanted Gavin to fuck me.

"Do you have any idea how much I love kissing you?" Gavin said between kisses.

"I happen to love kissing you, too."

"Good," Gavin said with a chuckle. "It would have been awkward if you didn't."

"I don't think I couldn't. You're a good kisser."

"I haven't been told that since I was in college."

"You've been kissing the wrong girls, then."

"Oh God, have I," Gavin muttered.

I wrapped my arms around his neck, and he pulled me against him, his hand flat on my back. He made me feel small and delicate when he held me. His body was large and muscular, and his hands were capable. I shivered as he held me, knowing what his hands could do.

Gavin nibbled on my lip. He slid his hand down and cupped my ass, using the leverage to grind himself against me. I whimpered. Gavin wound my hair around his free hand, his fingers against my scalp, and he tugged lightly so that I looked up at him. His hazel eyes were dark, filled with a need that mirrored my own. I breathed hard through parted lips and slid my eyes back to his mouth.

Gavin made a primal growling sound, and he moved his face to my neck. He nibbled my earlobe, and goosebumps spread down my neck and down my shoulder. He sucked my earlobe into his mouth, and I let out a gasping giggle. It tickled, and it was so fucking hot at the same time.

Gavin moved down my neck, leaving a trail of kisses in his wake. He let go of my ass and cupped my breast instead. My nipples were erect, pushing up against the lace bra. Gavin ran his thumb over one nipple for a moment before he let go and pushed his hand under my shirt. He tugged the cup of my bra down and rolled my nipple between his thumb and forefinger. The attention on my breasts sent electric shocks of pure lust to my pussy.

"Gavin," I moaned.

He stopped, tugged my cup back up and retrieved his hand.

"Come with me."

He took my hand and led me down a set of very tall stairs into the belly of the boat.

Everything about this boat screamed luxury. I'd thought the deck had been fancy. Down here, everything was decorated with plush carpets with a pine and beige color scheme. Gavin led me through a small office area with state-of-the-art technology, a living room section, a very modern kitchen, and finally, the sleeping area. I couldn't call it a bedroom—the bed took up most of the space. A large television dominated one wall.

Gavin pulled me against him and kissed me again. His tongue slid into my mouth, tasting and probing, and he laid me down on the bed. He pushed one leg between my thighs, pressing against my pussy, and he pinned me down. He tugged up my shirt, moving tantalizingly slowly. I watched his face as he unwrapped me, revealing my bare skin.

For a moment, I was worried he would know I was pregnant. I wasn't showing yet, but my stomach wasn't as flat as it had been before.

Gavin didn't say anything, and when he'd gotten rid of my shirt—I lifted myself up so he could tug it over my head before I fell back onto the pillows—he stared at my breasts with lust in his eyes.

"You're so fucking beautiful," he said, and his eyes met mine. "You have no idea what you do to me."

He tugged at my bra strap, pulling it off my shoulder. I arched my back and undid the clasp behind me with one hand. Gavin pulled off my bra and tossed it to the side. He dipped his head and circled my right nipple with his tongue. I let out a long moan. Gavin took it as the encouragement it was and sucked my nipple into his mouth. While he sucked, he ran his fingers up the side of my body, and I shivered and trembled.

I gyrated my hips, rubbing myself against his leg that was still pressed up against me. I wanted him so badly. Gavin grinded himself against me, his thick flesh hard and hot on my stomach.

"I should have told you how I felt sooner," he said, gasping as we grinded against each other. "We could have done a lot more of this."

I smiled at him. "You told me tonight, and we're doing this now."

Gavin kissed me again before he sat back and pulled his shirt over his head. I stared at his body. I'd seen him naked a few times before, but I could never get enough of his chiseled chest, his sculpted abs, and the way his muscles rippled under his skin when he moved. He was a god, and I wanted to worship every inch of his body with my tongue.

I lifted my head and kissed Gavin's chest. I moved around, planting kisses, licking the skin, tasting him.

Gavin moaned and gently pushed me down onto the mattress again. I shivered. I loved it when he took control like this.

He pulled down my leggings, rolling them over my legs like he was unwrapping a present. His face was desperate with need, and my breath came in ragged gasps. I sucked my bottom lip into my mouth.

When Gavin had got rid of my leggings and my panties, he wasn't fucking around—he moved back up my body and kissed me. He sucked my lower lip into his mouth, scraping his teeth against it. While he kissed me, he parted my legs and pushed his fingers into my slit. I writhed on the bed, gasping when he flicked his fingers over my clit. Gavin planted one more kiss on my lips before he moved down my body. He kissed my breasts, my stomach, and finally, he planted a kiss on my pubic bone.

"Gavin!" I cried out when he pushed his tongue into my slit and licked a line from my entrance to my clit. I pushed my hands into his hair, gyrating my hips. Gavin put a hand on my hip to steady me and sucked my clit into his mouth. He alternated between licking and sucking, and I moaned and whimpered, reduced to a puddle of need on the bed.

He moved down my pussy and pushed his tongue into my entrance. He replaced his tongue with two fingers and moved back to my clit.

He pushed me closer and closer to the edge of an orgasm, and when he stroked his fingers in and out of me, the pleasure exploded. My body contracted, and I cried out. I closed my legs around Gavin's head and bucked my hips against his mouth. A wash of ecstasy ran through me, taking my breath away.

When I came down from the sexual high, I gasped and moaned, and heat spread through my body. I shuddered when the orgasm was over and glanced down at Gavin, who smiled up at me from between my legs.

He crawled up my body again and kissed me, and I tasted myself on his lips. I tugged at his pants, undoing his belt buckle, and he helped me, wriggling them down. He got off the bed to kick off his shoes and his pants, and I stared at his cock, large, rock hard, and the head slick with need.

I shifted on the bed until he stood between my legs, and without ceremony, I sucked him into my mouth. Gavin had planned this night to woo me, to make me feel special, and he could keep doing that in just a second. I just wanted to taste him, to give him pleasure the same way he'd given me. I bobbed my head back and forth, stroking him in and out of my mouth. Gavin bit out a groan and ran his fingers through my hair.

"You're going to make me lose it, and I don't want this to be over," he said in a thick voice and pulled back. He bent down and kissed me, wrapping his arm around my waist. He crawled onto the bed and pulled me up with him until we were back where we'd started.

He positioned his cock at my entrance, and my legs fell open for him. He pressed his mouth against mine when he pushed into me, and I cried out against his lips. He lowered himself onto his elbows so that my breasts pushed up against his chest, and he rocked his hips, pushing deeper and deeper into me.

"Oh, shit," he muttered and froze inside me. "I'm not wearing a condom."

"It's fine." I gasped.

Gavin stayed frozen for a second longer before he started moving inside me again. I cried out as he fucked me harder and harder, his thick cock ramming deeper and deeper with every thrust.

The sex was better than it had ever been before. I loved feeling him without a condom. I closed my eyes, getting lost in the sensation.

Gavin pounded into me, and I cried out in rhythm with our fucking. Yes, yes, yes! This was what I wanted. Not just because we were horny and wanted to get off, but because I wanted Gavin—physically and emotionally and every other way I could have a man in my life.

"Wait," Gavin said and pulled out of me. I whimpered, feeling his absence acutely. My body ached for a release. "We can't do this. You feel fantastic, but…" He found his wallet and produced a condom. I groaned in frustration. "Rather safe than sorry, right?"

Fuck, he didn't want kids. He'd told me that. He would stand by that, no matter what. I should have been pleased that he was responsible. So few guys were, and Gavin really made a point of doing the right thing.

Even if it wouldn't make a difference. We'd worn a condom before, and I'd still gotten pregnant, and now…

Gavin came back to me, all wrapped up, and he slid into me again. I stopped thinking about the future, about what would happen when I had to leave, about how this would eventually play out and focused on the now.

That was all that mattered. Tomorrow, I would face the rest of my life again. Right now, Gavin and I were in love, and his cock inside me felt like heaven.

He slid in and out of me again, pulling out and pushing in, and I moved with him. I bucked my hips and held onto his thick shoulders for dear life as he fucked me. I cried out, and Gavin's face was tense with concentration—he was holding back so this could last longer.

Just because he was holding back didn't mean I had to, and I orgasmed a second time. I cried out and trembled as my body tightened around his cock, squeezing him.

Gavin cussed through gritted teeth before he kissed me again. He pushed up on his arms and picked up his pace, fucking me harder. I moaned as it drew out my orgasm, extending the pleasure. I curled my fingers, digging them into his skin, and I felt myself pulsate around his cock.

"Fuck, Paige," Gavin bit out, and a moment later, he pushed into me as deep as he could go. His cock kicked inside me as he released, and I cried out, feeling the orgasm wash through his body. His muscles rippled and contracted, his cock pulsated inside me, and he breathed hard, dropping his head into my neck so that I heard him groaning and gasping. I slid one hand behind his head and into his hair, and with the other, I held onto his shoulder, and Gavin's large body covered mine.

His orgasm seemed to last forever, and I was still bathing in the aftermath of mine, and then, slowly, it all faded. Gavin gasped for air. I breathed hard, our chests rising and falling against each other, and I felt lightheaded. Gavin collapsed his arms and lay on me for a moment. He nuzzled my neck before he rolled off me, letting up so that I could breathe.

"You're everything," he said in a deep voice. The statement was so soft, I barely heard it, but the words were there, and I shivered. "I'm so glad you feel the same way about me."

"I've felt this way about you for a while."

I felt him smile.

Warmth filled my body. Knowing he cared about me the same way I cared about him was an amazing feeling. Uncertainty followed on its heels, but I pushed it away. I had all the time in the world to panic about my future. Right now, I wanted to relish in our closeness and in the fact that, at least for a short while, everything was perfect.

21

Gavin

Everything had worked out as I'd hoped. In fact, it had worked out better than I'd hoped.

Paige and I were together.

At least, we'd told each other how we felt about each other, and it was a lot more than just being friends and doing this thing together where we tricked the rest of the world into believing that I was a better person than Tara had painted me to be.

We hadn't actually defined who and what we were to each other, but that would come in due time.

Right now, everything was perfect, and I didn't want to rock the boat too much.

We still had a lot of talking to do. I wanted to be with Paige, and with her going back to Seattle eventually, that didn't work. I wanted her with me. She needed a job, but that was an easy fix—I could have her work at the company. I didn't have a large company that I owned and acted as the CEO of for nothing. It was high time I used my resources to do something for myself for a change.

She needed a place to live, but that was easy to take care of, too.

She could stay with me. In my room, rather than a spare bedroom.

The rest of it was a formality. There was nothing to make official to the rest of the world because they already believed that we were together.

I stood in the grocery store, trying to find the right ingredients for a recipe I wanted to try to make for Paige. I scrolled on my phone for the list of ingredients I'd saved somewhere.

"Gavin?"

When I looked up, Tara was standing in front of me. Her blonde hair had been cut shorter, her lips were a deep red, and she wore some kind of runway outfit that looked out of place in the grocery store.

"Oh my God, this is the last place I thought I'd see you."

"Everyone eats," I said with a shrug.

She giggled even though it wasn't that funny.

"Yeah, I guess that's true... how have you been?"

"Fine," I glanced around, looking for a way to escape.

"That's good, that's good..." She nodded and hesitated for a moment before she kept going. "Are we never going to talk again?"

"We don't really have anything to say to each other."

"That's not true. We shared a life together for three years, Gav. Doesn't that mean anything?"

I didn't answer her. She sighed.

"I wish we could just put this nasty business behind us and be friends."

"I don't think we can be friends."

"Why not?"

"Because that's not what you want," I said flatly. "You want more, and I'm not willing to give you more."

Tara's lips curled into a smile, but her eyes shimmered like she was going to cry.

"We don't always get what we want, right? I still want to be in your life."

I shook my head. "After everything we've been through, I don't think that's going to work. Especially not with Paige in my life. It's time you moved on, too."

"I didn't realize you were that serious about her," Tara said softly. "I thought she was a rebound—"

"She's not."

Tara shook her head and reached for the apples on the shelf next to us. She squeezed them absently.

"What do you see in her?" she asked, turning her bright-blue eyes to me. "How can you be so happy with her so soon?"

"Some people just work together. It's not something I planned, it just happened." All of it was true.

"Shit like that only happens in books and movies," Tara scoffed. "You're just trying to get in the public's good graces." Her expression changed from vulnerable and emotional to cold and hard. "You don't give a shit about who she is; you just want what you can get from her. You've always been like that."

"No, Tara, that's what *you're* like."

She laughed bitterly. "That's not fair. I really loved you. *Love*. I still love you, Gavin. Why don't you just let me show you?"

It was my turn to laugh bitterly. "For someone who claims you love me so much, you have a bullshit way of showing it. You tried to tank my reputation, you tried to make my life hell—"

"I was upset about losing you! Haven't you ever been beside your-self with grief? When I lost you, I didn't know what I was thinking, what I was doing. If you hadn't dump—"

I raised my eyebrows at her. "Don't you dare tell me it was my fault that you lashed out at me. You didn't have to act like a spoiled brat."

"I just wanted to save what we had."

"We didn't have anything!" I cried out. "What I have with Paige is real, and it's taught me so much about what love is meant to be."

Tara laughed sarcastically. "Don't use words you don't understand, Gavin. You can't possibly love her. It won't last with this woman, and when it's over—"

"We're engaged."

Tara paled. "What?"

Shit. I shouldn't have said that but who the fuck was Tara to tell me what I felt and what my choices should have been? I wanted her to know I was happy without her. I wanted her to understand.

"That's how happy I am with her, and that's how long it's going to last," I added. Fuck if I wasn't going to man up and mean what I said. I wanted Paige in my life long-term, anyway. What did it matter if we weren't engaged yet? Maybe Tara would finally understand and leave me alone.

"I have to go," I said shaking my head.

Tara looked like she was going to have some kind of meltdown, her face scrunched up as if searching for the right words to make me stay. The last thing I needed was to be around her when that happened. It would just be another public outburst that would end up all over the internet.

Especially if it involved her.

I wasn't going to let Tara ruin my happiness ever again.

"Gavin," she said in a small voice when I turned and walked away from her. I didn't turn back to see the expression on her face, to see how she would deal with the news. I had a wonderful woman to get home to, someone I wanted to be in my life for a long, long time.

It was time to focus on the future and not keep looking back at the darkness in my past.

22

Paige

"I'm fine, Mom," I said on the phone. "I'm just staying a bit longer than I thought I would, but I'll be home soon. I'll let you know the moment I am."

"Something doesn't seem right here, honey," Mom said. "What about your job? This isn't like you, staying away for so long, not taking care of your responsibilities."

I rolled my eyes. "I'm fine. My boss is okay with this, and I don't have to justify what I'm doing. I don't need cash, and I don't need a lecture."

Mom sighed. "I'm not lecturing you. I'm just worried you'll get hurt. It looks like you and this Gavin man are very close, and to tell me the whole thing is a lie…"

It wasn't a lie anymore.

"I'm just helping out a friend."

"That's something you do too much of," Mom said.

"You're telling me I'm helping too much?" I asked with a laugh.

"At your own expense, yeah. You are."

"I'm really going to be just fine, Mom. It's not going to last forever, and then I'm back home, and everything will be back to normal."

Sort of.

The moment I returned to Seattle, I would have a whole new topic to discuss with my mom, and then she would *really* be worried, but I wasn't going to cross that bridge right now. I wasn't going to break the news to her about the baby over the phone, and I meant it when I told her I would be okay. I knew heartbreak waited for me, but at least expecting it gave me the leverage to deal with it rather than the heartache coming out of the blue.

I heard the front door open.

"I have to go, Mom. We'll talk soon."

I ended the call and walked to the living room. Gavin put his bag down at the door, tossed his wallet and keys onto the table, and smiled at me.

"You're a sight for sore eyes," he said and came to me. He wrapped his arms around me and kissed me. "How was your day?"

"It was fine," I said. "Not much to report. I spent a lot of time binge-watching series and eating snacks." I didn't add that I'd spent the better part of the day hugging the toilet, with my body ejecting all the snacks again. Apparently, the little one growing inside me had protested against what I'd put in my body.

"I had an eventful day," Gavin said with a grin. "Do you want something to drink?"

"Coffee, if you're making."

"Sure."

I followed Gavin to the kitchen and sat down at the breakfast nook. I felt drained today, and standing too long made me feel lightheaded. At some point, I was going to have to book a doctor's appointment and get some prenatal meds, a checkup to make sure the baby was okay, stuff like that. I wouldn't do that until I was back in Seattle.

"I ran into Tara in the grocery store."

"Oh, wow," I said. "That *is* eventful. You don't have any groceries with you."

"Yeah, I wanted to get away from her before she had a meltdown and implicated me in some way, so I just left my basket in the aisle and got the hell out of dodge. What do you want to drink?"

"Decaf."

"I don't see what you like about decaf, it's like drinking virgin cocktails. No point at all."

I shrugged, and Gavin put a decaf pod in the machine before pushing buttons, and the machine got to work producing my cup of coffee.

"What did she want?" I asked.

"She went on about how we belong together, and we have three years behind us that I can't throw away. She told me you and I won't ever last because you're just a rebound."

I giggled. "I guess it could be construed that way."

Gavin snorted. "Yeah, I guess. It's not a rebound if I haven't been emotionally invested in a hell of a long time, though. It was just going through the motions with her for ages. Not that I'm going to share that with the press or convince her or anything."

"Right," I said. "What did you say to her when she said I was a rebound?"

"I told her she's wrong. I told her we're engaged."

Blood drained from my face, and my ears burned hot.

"What?"

"I didn't want her to think we don't mean anything."

"So you told her we're *engaged*?" I couldn't believe what I was hearing.

"Yeah... it just slipped out, but it's not a bad thing. She gets how serious this is."

I shook my head and squeezed my eyes shut for a moment, trying to calm my racing pulse.

"It's not that serious, Gavin."

Gavin brought me the cup of coffee he'd made for me.

"Well, not yet, it's not," Gavin said and grinned at me. "But she doesn't have to know that."

"You can't just go around telling people we're engaged."

Gavin looked confused. "Why not? That's how this thing with you pretending to be my girlfriend started."

That was true—I'd been the one to tell Tara we were together.

"It's not the same thing. I was helping you out of a bind."

"It's just one person," Gavin countered and put a pod into the machine for his own coffee. "So what if she thinks we're engaged? If it will make her leave me alone—"

"What about me?"

Gavin frowned. "What about you?"

I gasped, incredulous. "I don't have a say in this?"

"I didn't mean it that way," Gavin said quickly. "What if that's where we're headed, anyway?"

"How can you know that?" I demanded. "We've only been doing this a couple of weeks. We don't know that much about each other, and telling the world we're engaged is very different from them believing we're together for the sake of your image." My voice rose the more I talked. I felt cornered—sure, Gavin was a great guy, and I knew how he felt about me, but *engaged*?

"I don't understand what you're so upset about," Gavin said.

His coffee finished, but he didn't make a move to pick up the cup. I hadn't touched my coffee, either.

"This is going way too fast," I said. Not to mention the fact that I knew it was destined to end.

"It's just something I said, Paige," Gavin said, defending his actions.

"You can't use that as justification! You can't just say shit and think it doesn't have any repercussions. Besides, you said it to *Tara*. That woman has the ability to really fuck things up for you if she wants to, and even if she doesn't, they'll listen to her if she says something. If it ends up in the press…"

Gavin leaned against the counter and folded his arms over his chest. He was getting pissed off. I was already there—I was furious.

"I didn't think I had to ask you before I made decisions about my life," Gavin said tightly.

"It's not just your life in question here," I snapped. "It's my life, too."

"We're together!" Gavin cried out. "Is it really that bad if the world thinks we're engaged?"

"Are we ever going to be allowed to make our own decisions and not care what the rest of the world thinks?" I asked. "Or will public opinion always influence where this is going between us? Since it's already defined our relationship, maybe we should run a public poll and give them the majority of the vote." The last words were delivered with a big dollop of sarcasm.

Gavin narrowed his eyes at me. "You're making me sound like I'm not allowing us anything private."

"You're not!"

"What could be so bad that the world isn't allowed to know about it?"

"It's not that," I said. My throat swelled shut, and my eyes stung with tears. How was this happening? I struggled to breathe. I felt like

I was being tied down, and no matter what I said and did, none of my life belonged to me anymore.

"Then what is it?"

"I just want to be able to talk to you, have a relationship without Melissa and your board of directors and your prospective clients hanging in the balance. I want to be able to discuss things in private."

"You can."

"I can't! You might just run to Tara with it."

"You're pulling it out of proportion," Gavin scoffed.

I stilled. "Are you fucking kidding me?"

"I don't get what you're so pissed about."

"I'm pissed you're not giving me a say! I'm pissed because I have no control over what's happening, and everything I once had is slipping through my fingers. I'm pissed because you're forcing me into something I can't give you."

"What does that even mean?" Gavin asked.

"I'm pregnant," I blurted out.

Gavin froze and stared at me.

"What did you say?"

23

Paige

He stared at me like I'd just upended everything he thought to be true. Maybe he hadn't heard me right.

"I'm pregnant, Gavin," I said again.

He shook his head like he was trying to make sense of what I'd just said.

"We're having a baby?" His voice was thin and a pitch higher than it had been a moment ago.

I nodded.

"And it's mine?"

"What?" I cried out.

Of all the fucking accusations he could throw at a woman, suggesting that she slept around and didn't know who the father was was the *worst* thing he could possibly throw at me.

"That's not what I meant. God." He pressed his fingers to his temples. "I don't get how this happened. I always use protection. *Always*. So that this doesn't fucking happen. How—" He glared at me. "You wanted to do it without a condom the other night! I can't believe this. I put one on. I thought it would be safe. Fuck, Paige!"

"I'm in my second trimester."

Gavin frowned. "What?"

Maybe he didn't know what that meant.

"I'm just over twelve weeks pregnant."

Gavin shook his head like I was talking a different language.

"I didn't get pregnant because you didn't have a condom on for that short little bit. I was already pregnant by then. That's why I didn't care about the condom. I got pregnant from the first time."

Gavin frowned. "That's not possible."

"Condoms aren't a hundred percent foolproof."

"Aren't you on some form of birth control?"

"That's not always guaranteed, either. Shit happens, okay? The point is, I'm pregnant."

Gavin looked like he was going to faint. He made a strange motion with his mouth and rubbed the back of his neck with a flat hand.

"I can't do this," he finally said.

"I know."

"What do you mean, you know? You have no fucking idea what this means."

"Don't tell me I don't know what it means," I shot back.

"Why didn't you tell me?"

"That's what I came to do when we decided I would pose as your girlfriend. It wasn't supposed to go this way, but then Melissa was going on about what a good idea it was, and you seemed so stuck..."

"I never asked you to help me," Gavin snapped.

"Excuse me?" I said, incredulous. "That's *exactly* what you did! You begged me to help you out, so I did, and I didn't say anything about the baby."

Gavin shook his head back and forth, back and forth. He muttered more to himself than me, and I watched him put all the pieces together—me throwing up, me not drinking alcohol.

"Do you have any idea what the public will do if they figure this out? My stocks will crash. The tabloids will rip into me. Tara will have a field day. Fuck, she'll lose her mind. I can't have a baby."

My stomach dropped to my shoes as he rambled on about his public image. Right. This wasn't even about Gavin not being ready for a baby. This was about his image. Then again, I was here for his image, too. It was the reason I hadn't told him in the first place.

"I thought maybe things would be different now," I said. "I thought after it was all over, we could just be us and not worry about the rest of the world."

Gavin paced the kitchen, hands on his hips.

"Were you *ever* going to tell me?" he asked, looking at me.

"Yeah." I sighed. "No."

"So, what did you think I would do when you had the baby?"

"I wasn't going to be around that long."

Gavin stopped in his tracks, spun around and stared at me. It was hard to figure out the expression on his face, but it wasn't a good one. "You were just going to dump me and leave?"

"I didn't think you cared about me that way!"

"Well, I do."

A flicker of hope ignited inside me. He cared about me, and now he knew about the baby. It hadn't come out the way I'd wanted it to, but at least he knew now. Maybe we could find a way to make this work after all. Maybe, like Ava had said, he would feel differently now that it wasn't just a theory anymore.

"You should have told me sooner," Gavin said, scrubbing his hands down his face.

"Would you have felt differently?"

Gavin shook his head.

"I didn't think so," I said tightly. "Look, I get it. You don't want kids, you said so yourself, and that's fine. After this is over, I'm going back to Seattle, and you won't have to be involved."

"You want to take the baby away from me?"

"You don't want the baby!" I cried out.

"I never said that."

"You told me you never want kids when I told you about Ava."

"That's not what I said. It's just… it's a fucked up world, Paige."

"Yeah, and we're having a baby. There's no stopping it now. This is happening. You don't have to like it."

Gavin shook his head. He was frustrated and furious. He was allowed to be—I'd had some time to process it, where this news was still fresh to him.

"Look, I think I'm going to Ava's for a couple of days. Let me know when you want to talk, and we can go through this step-by-step."

"I can't be a father, Paige," Gavin said in a strained voice. "You don't get it."

I stood and walked toward the kitchen door. I hadn't touched my coffee at all.

"I'm not asking you to be a father. A lot of kids grow up without them. I'll figure this out on my own."

Gavin leaned against the counter as if his legs wouldn't hold him up anymore.

"You get why I can't be involved, right? Not after what my dad did to me. He was never there, and I—"

"And you're choosing not to be there, too."

Gavin scowled. "That's not what I'm saying."

"I'm going to go to Ava's and let you take some time to let the news sink in," I said. "We're just going to say things we don't mean if we go on fighting about it now. Take the time to cool off, and—"

"Don't come back," Gavin said. His voice was cold.

"What?" I blinked at him, shocked.

"You heard me. When you pack to go to Ava's, take everything because I don't want you to come back. I can't do this."

"You're dumping me?"

"Yeah."

"After you told me you're in love with me."

"I didn't know you were pregnant, then."

I gasped, horrified. His words sliced through me like a knife.

"I didn't realize your love was conditional."

"Don't make me out to be the bad guy."

"You're dumping me because I'm pregnant with your baby. How does that make you the *good* guy?"

Gavin shook his head without responding.

"You know what?" I said, anger and hurt swirling in my chest. "Maybe Tara had a right to be as upset as she was when you kicked her out."

Gavin stared at me in disbelief. "You did not just say that."

"If this is how your emotions work, if you can flip them off and on like a switch, then I feel for her. Maybe there are more sides to this story than you're making it seem."

Gavin looked like he was going to explode. I didn't care. He had just dumped me, and I was done with being nice to him. I marched out of the kitchen to pack. I swallowed hard to try to get rid of the lump in my throat, but tears spilled onto my cheeks anyway.

Damn it, I'd known this wouldn't be forever. I'd known it would end.

I just hadn't thought he would be the one to dump me.
I just hadn't thought it would hurt so fucking much.

24

Gavin

F uck, fuck, fuck.

Fuck!

How the hell did this happen? One minute I was head over heels in love and ready to spend the foreseeable future with a woman who loved me back. The next, I was the father of an unborn child and single again.

Paige had some nerve to tell me Tara had a point! Who the hell did she think she was? She didn't know Tara. She hadn't been here to see what had happened.

She had a point, though. I'd kicked her out, breaking it off, telling her to leave rather than facing this mess head-on. I just couldn't do it. Paige wouldn't ever understand what it was all about. She had a wonderful, loving family. She'd had a great example of what a perfect family had to look like, how parents loved each other and their kids. She could define a happy ending and aim for one because she'd actually seen it.

I couldn't be a dad. The only example I had was my MIA alcohol dad, who'd only ever used me and my mom to get what he wanted. He'd spent more of his life with us drunk than sober.

How could I be a supportive father? How could I be a loving family man? The only thing I knew how to do well was run a business, and having a family and kids was *nothing* like that.

I got in my car and tried to figure out where to go. I wanted to drink. A *lot*. That wasn't going to work, though. If I drowned my sorrows now, I wasn't going to stop at a reasonable time, and I would get shitfaced and wind up in the paper again. My reputation was doing so well—thanks to Paige—and now that I'd chased her out of my life, it was all I had left.

Hell, my business and my reputation were all I'd *ever* really had. Everything else in my life had been seasonal. I'd been a fucking fool to think that this thing with Paige could mean more. Nothing lasted when it was worth something in my life.

I headed in a direction and ended up in front of Parker and Emily's place. I took out my phone and dialed Parker.

"Are you home?" I asked.

"Yeah."

"I'm at your gate. Do you have time for a drink?"

"Where?"

"At your bar. There's less chance of any paparazzi finding me there."

"Sure," Parker said, and the gate opened automatically a moment later.

When I got out of my car, Parker met me at the front door.

"You look like shit," he said with a grin.

"Thanks, asshole."

The smile faded from his face. "What happened?"

"Paige is pregnant."

"Jesus," Parker said and stepped aside, leading me into the house. I led the way to his bar, not even bothering to find Emily and the kids to say hello, first.

"What happened?" Parker asked when he stepped behind his bar and poured me a glass of whiskey. He didn't just pour in two or three fingers, he filled it all the way to the top. Good. He knew he would just have to keep refilling it otherwise.

I gulped down the whiskey like it was water, and Parker watched me with raised eyebrows.

"Tell me what happened."

"We fucked, the condom failed, and now she has a baby on the way."

"Thanks for that," Parker said sarcastically. "I didn't mean how she got pregnant, I meant the rest of it. How did you find out?"

I sighed and pushed my glass toward Parker for a refill, telling him how everything had gone down.

"You broke up with her," Parker echoed when I finished my story.

I nodded. "Yeah."

"What the fuck were you thinking?"

I gasped. "What?"

"You find out she's pregnant and the first thing you do is kick her out. Fuck, Gavin, what the hell is wrong with you?"

I bristled. "It's not like she's on the streets. Besides, she offered to go."

"To let you cool down so you can talk when you've gotten used to the idea. Wasn't that what you just said?"

"What was I supposed to do?"

Parker shook his head, sipping his own tumbler of whiskey. He'd only poured two fingers for himself. He was always in control, wise, and able to be the good guy. That was why he'd found his fucking happy ending. People like Parker just pissed me off.

"You were supposed to take the time to get used to the idea and then talk to her," Parker deadpanned. "That much is pretty clear."

I groaned. "She's fucking *pregnant*, Parker. With a *baby*."

Parker narrowed his eyes. "I know what it means, Gavin. Stop being a dick and making it sound like I'm stupid, and tell me why you think getting rid of her is the answer."

I shook my head. "I came here for advice, not a lecture."

"If this is how you were acting with her, no wonder she suggested you take some time to cool off."

I glared at him. "You're being an asshole."

Parker sipped his drink without answering, and I let out a deep sigh.

"I'm just not cut out for this," I said. "I'm not good in relationships, and I sure as shit won't be a good father."

"What's your definition of a good father?"

I shook my head. "That's just the thing. How the hell should I know?"

"You just have to be there, Gavin. Time and energy and love. That's all kids want from you, and it's easy to give when you know that's how it works. It happens to be how relationships last, too."

"I'm no good at any of those things. Tara was the person I dated the longest, and look how that worked out. I don't talk to my dad, and my mom lives in a dream world where her best advice is to take Tara back. I've been doing it on my own for this long for a reason."

"You're willing to lose Paige because of your past?"

I sighed. "I was going to lose her, anyway. She said she would have broken it off to go back to Seattle. It wasn't even meant to be in her mind."

Parker shook his head, and when I finished my whiskey, he poured more. Even when he didn't agree with me, even when he didn't think drinking until I stopped feeling was the right thing to do. Parker was there for me even when he thought I was an idiot, and I appreciated that about him.

At least I had good friends. That was something.

I wished things were different. I wished *I* was different. I wasn't, though. I was Gavin Austin, the man who made money because at least money wouldn't disappoint me.

More importantly, I couldn't disappoint money.

I knew Parker didn't get it, but I knew who I was and what it meant. Paige and the baby were both better off without me, even if she didn't think that was true. She knew about my past, but she didn't know enough, and she didn't know the future.

I'd hurt her, going on about my image as if that was what tripped me about this. The thing was, being a dad scared the living shit out of me, and when she'd told me, I'd gone into defense mode. It was the only way I knew how to deal with shit. I had to protect what I had, and what I had was my reputation and my business.

Even though Paige had done everything in her power to help me with my image. She wouldn't ever do anything to jeopardize it. Everything I'd said had come out so wrong, and I didn't know how to fix it.

I didn't *have* to fix it when there was nothing left to fix, I reminded myself.

"I'm going to say one thing on the topic, and then I'll shut up about it," Parker finally said.

"What?"

"Turning your back on your dad and leaving him behind when you were old enough wasn't a bad thing. You had to get yourself out of there. That doesn't mean running is the answer to every problem in your life."

I opened my mouth to argue, but Parker held up his hand to silence me.

"I'm just putting it out there. I don't want you to justify it, I'm just saying."

I snapped my mouth shut and sipped my whiskey. The edge of my vision was already getting fuzzy, and the bar started to spin. The satisfying numbness I'd been after would come soon.

It couldn't come soon enough. My chest hurt like someone had wedged a knife between my ribs.

The kicker was that someone had been me.

It hurt like a bitch losing Paige. It hadn't hurt to get rid of Tara, but with Paige, everything had been different from day one. The thing was, it would have hurt at some point, even if I tried sticking it out and going through with it. I would inevitably fuck it up.

This way, it was over and done. Expectation management was the name of the game, right? Now, Paige expected me not to be there, so I couldn't disappoint, and I expected to be alone for the rest of my life.

I was good at that.

Ending it with Paige had been like ripping off a Band-Aid. It had hurt, but it was over, and now she could move on, and she would be okay.

As for where it left me... did it fucking matter?

25

Paige

I cried all the way to the airport. Ava sat next to me in the driver's seat, and she didn't know what to say.

"Is there no way you can talk to him?" she asked for the hundredth time.

"And say what? He made it clear he doesn't want this, and I knew it would be this way." I sniveled and wiped my cheeks with my sleeves. "I'd known this was coming. It just hurts so fucking much to know that it wasn't about me, about the baby, but about *him*."

Ava shook her head. "Something doesn't add up. It's not how I know Gavin."

"It's how *I* know him."

After all, he'd said he didn't want kids, right? He'd told me straight up that it wasn't the life he wanted. That night when he'd told me he was in love with me, I should have told him it was better if we just stayed friends. I shouldn't have accepted it, slept with him... I shouldn't have entertained the idea that we could make something of this, after all.

It would never have worked out.

"Thank you for bringing me," I said in a thick voice when Ava parked the car in the drop-off zone.

"Of course. I just wish I could do more to help."

"You're my best friend, you're always there for me. That's all I need." I leaned over and hugged her. We held onto each other for a long time before she finally let go.

"Are you going to be okay?"

"I'll be okay," I said. "I have my family, and I can do this. A lot of moms are doing it alone now."

"That doesn't mean it should be that way," Ava said.

I nodded, and with a pang of envy, I thought about when she'd gotten pregnant at first, and Noah had leaped to be at her side and make it work. I wished I'd had that happy ending, too. It didn't work out that way for everyone, though.

"We totally get to be pregnant together, and that's something to look forward to," I said, forcing a smile. "And we'll just have to meet up for playdates when we get to that point."

Ava smiled and nodded, going with the rosy mental image I tried to paint to make it seem like everything would be just fine.

It would be—it was up to me to make it happen, and that was exactly what I was going to do.

Somehow.

"Call me when you land so I know you're safe."

I nodded and got out of the car to get my bags from the trunk.

Ava hugged me one more time before I headed into the airport alone. I didn't want Ava to wait with me until I boarded. She had a family to get back to, and she deserved every minute she could get with them. This was my journey, and I had to travel it alone.

The thought of losing Gavin made me burst into tears again.

When I arrived at the check-in counter, the woman behind the counter looked at me, concerned.

"Tough goodbye?"

"You have no idea."

"It's hard leaving your family behind."

That only made me cry harder, and she got flustered, not knowing what to do or say.

We went through the motions of getting my ticket printed and my bags checked, and finally I walked to the plastic chairs in the waiting area where I would wait for my flight to board.

It was good I was going back home to my support network. My mom would be there for me. My baby would grow up surrounded by aunts and uncles and cousins who loved him or her, and my parents would dote on the baby.

Just because I didn't get what I wanted didn't mean the baby wouldn't get what it deserved—all the love in the world.

When the boarding call sounded, I got up and walked to the stewardess with my ticket.

"Going home?" she asked.

I nodded. "Yeah."

"It's always good to be home. Have a safe flight, honey."

I thanked her and boarded the plane.

I was going to Seattle, but for some twisted reason, it didn't feel like I was going home.

LA had become home. Gavin had become home.

And I was leaving it behind.

"Welcome to *Metropolitan Prime*, where you'll find the latest celebrity news—and gossip—as it happens! I'm your host, Kieran Cohen, and joining me tonight for the updates you've all been waiting for is Tara Logan!"

The audience erupted in applause, and Tara walked out from backstage, smiling and waving at everyone. She sat down next to Kieran, casually kicking off her shoes and tucking her feet under her on the leather couch.

"Getting comfortable, I see," Kieran said with a smile.

"I feel so at home here," Tara said. "I love coming onto the show. It always feels like I'm meeting up with close friends."

The audience lost their mind at that statement, and Tara smiled, a blush creeping onto her cheeks. She

hooked her blonde hair behind one ear with mani-
cured nails.

"Tell us how you've been," Kieran said.

Tara let out a shaky breath. "I won't lie to you, Kieran. I've been better. Getting over real heartbreak is a
process, you know? There isn't a statute of limitations
on it—although I wish there was."

"It does take time to deal with the aftermath," Kieran
said, nodding sympathetically. "You had the chance to
find love on the most recent game show that aired just
the other day, but you turned down a suitor and left
the show, shocking the world and all your fans to the
core. Can you tell me why you chose to do that?"

Tara pursed her lips together. "I guess I just wasn't
ready to move on, you know? It's not right to draw
someone into a relationship and ask them to give me
their heart when I wasn't ready to do the same. I mean,
I know all too well how it feels to be the recipient in
a situation like that, so..." Her voice trailed off as her
eyes filled with tears.

"Gavin Austin has moved on," Kieran said. "Don't you think that it's time for you to do it, too?"

"I thought it was," Tara said. "It's what people expect, isn't it? They always say the right person will come, and I guess for a lot of people, that's true. It just isn't for me. Don't get me wrong"—she glanced at the audience—"everyone I met on that show was incredible, and they would make wonderful life partners, but I just wasn't ready for that. It's hard to offer something of yourself when it's broken and bent. It's just not fair."

"What are you going to do now?" Kieran asked. "What's in the stars for you, my dear?"

"I don't know," Tara said. "I'll just have to see where fate takes me. Maybe, one day, I will find the strength to try again. Maybe, Gavin and I will end up together again."

"Would you want that, after all he's put you through?" Kieran asked.

"Of course. I mean, I love him, you know? It's not something you can unlearn. You can't choose who you love, and I guess I'm cursed to love Gavin Austin no matter how terrible he can be."

"The heart wants what it wants."

Tara nodded and offered a teary smile. "He's my kryptonite."

The camera closed in on Kieran Cohen.

"There you have it, ladies and gentlemen. Love doesn't play favorites, does it? Thank you for joining us on *Metropolitan Prime*, where we keep it real."

—ele—

26

Gavin

I snorted and downed the rest of my whiskey.

"Can someone change this bullshit?" I asked the bartender.

"Yeah, sure," he said and flipped the channel to some stupid sports game. Anything was better than watching Tara Logan act like she was a victim of love.

"She has no end, does she?" Parker asked.

"No, she doesn't," I said and waved for another drink. "She's set on ruining me. She'll keep making it seem like I fucked up her life so badly until she gets what she wants."

"What does she want?"

"Who knows, at this point," I said and dropped my head onto the bar. "Money, fame, sympathy... to see me crash and burn... I don't know. All of the above."

"It won't last forever."

I groaned. The bartender returned with my drink.

"Just leave the fucking bottle, will you?"

The bartender did as I asked and shrugged.

"Everyone keeps saying that, but it's not true," I said to Parker. "It *will* last forever. Do you know how I know?"

"How?"

"She's like a stray that just won't go away. She's some kind of lock-jaw mongrel that won't let go the moment she has a good hold on something, and she decided that I'm the person she needs to be with, or she'll die trying to make sure that no one else will ever get a piece of me."

Anger swirled in my chest. I was furious with Tara for screwing everything up for me.

"I should never, ever have dated her. Why didn't I listen to you? Everyone was there, telling me that she was a walking red flag. Did I listen? No. Because Gavin fucking Austin doesn't like being told what to do."

Parker shook his head. "You're a jackass, you know that?"

I blinked at him, confused. "What?"

"Look at you. You're an angry, drunken mess. It's not because of Tara, though, no matter how you decide to blame her for it. You're doing exactly what she's doing."

I stared at Parker. "What did you just say to me?"

"Come on, man," Parker said. "It hurts like a bitch to hear it, but someone's gotta tell you the truth. You've been asking for her to fuck you up since the day you let her into your life because you're allowing yourself to be a victim of your circumstances just like she is."

My anger grew into a raging furnace in my chest, and it threatened to consume me. If I wasn't so drunk, I might have punched Parker in the face. My arms were *so* heavy, though.

"What the fuck is your problem?" I demanded instead.

"I know you're going through shit. Trust me, I've been there, but you can choose not to let this get to you, you know. Either you can let your past define you, or you can let it shape you."

I shook my head. "I didn't ask you to drink with me so that you could insult me and then give me fortune cookie advice. I'm not letting Tara define me, anyway."

"Not Tara, but your dad," Parker pointed out.

I glared at him. "I'm just about sick and tired of hearing about my past with my dad. I can't change who he is and what he did!"

"No, but you can stop letting it be the thing that ruins your life, you know. You're a mess because of what someone did when you were a kid. I get it. It's tough to let shit like that go. I held onto my dad's death as a reason for me not to get attached or involved for a long, long time. I nearly lost Emily because of it until I decided to pick myself up and stop being the victim. Shit happens, Gavin, but you can get up out of the ditch you're in, or you can stay in it and cry about it."

I shook my head. Through the waves of alcohol and the room spinning around me, Parker's words had a ring of truth to them. It pissed me off because I didn't like what I was hearing, but he wasn't wrong.

"Tara has a hold on you and your image and your money because you *don't* have a hold on it. Paige is pregnant with your child, and you're not doing anything about it because you don't want to be who your dad was. Looks to me like you hanging on the bar, drunk out of your brackets instead of facing the music, is exactly what you were trying to avoid. Don't prove them right, man."

I shook my head. It only made the world tilt on its axis, and I held onto the bar so I didn't fall off the barstool.

"So, what am I supposed to do?" I asked. I wanted to fight Parker. I wanted to ask him what kind of a best friend was so harsh. He wouldn't have been a best friend if he wasn't, though.

"Whatever it takes, Gavin," Parker said. "You want to be happy. You're the only person who can fix all this."

He was right. Damn it, he was right. I hated that I had to be the person to do it. It was so much easier blaming the rest of the world and feeling sorry for myself that my life wasn't what I wanted it to be, but it was up to me to do something about it.

My company hadn't built itself—I'd put in years of hard work. My life wasn't going to fix itself, either. I would have to face the facts and do something myself.

The difference between my company and my life was that my company had been an escape to get *away* from everything I hadn't wanted to face. If I decided to get up and face the music, I would have to turn back to the shit I'd been trying to get away from and face it head-on.

"Fuck you, Parker," I said, but my voice didn't come out hostile. Instead, I sounded exhausted.

"I know," Parker said. "It fucking hurts to hear it, but when you deal with it, you get to be happy, and that's worth it all. Trust me."

Parker had been through a hell of a lot, and his life was perfect now. Not because he'd had a good hand dealt to him or because luck favored him or because of anything other than the fact that he'd faced the hard times and fought for what he wanted.

What did I want?

To be free of Tara.

To be free of my father.

Paige.

I wanted her more than I dared to admit to my friends. They would think I was a fool for breaking things off with her.

"I have to go," Parker said. "Can I drop you off at home? Get you out of here in one piece?"

I looked over my shoulder at the door where the paparazzi were, no doubt waiting to get more scandalous photos of me that would only prove Tara right.

"Yeah. Thanks."

Parker nodded. We settled our bill and left the bar. Parker led me to his car, and the driver dropped me off at home. We didn't talk much in the car. Parker had had his say, and I had a lot of thinking to do. It was harder with the amount of alcohol in my system, but I was going home. I had to sober up, decide what mattered, and then I would change things so that I could get what I wanted.

Even if it scared me.

When Parker drove off, I waved at him before I turned into the building.

When the elevator doors slid open on the top floor, I already had my keys in my hand.

Tara was sitting on the floor in my foyer, her back against my front door.

"Gavin," she said when she saw me and got up. "You're here."

"What are you doing here?"

"Can we talk?"

27

Paige

Silence filled the space between us after I'd told my mom I was pregnant. I watched her expression as she carefully digested the information.

"Why didn't you tell me?" she finally asked.

"I had to figure out how I felt about it first," I said. "And I had a couple of things to take care of in LA."

"The Austin boy," Mom scoffed. "I know all about him."

I shook my head. "You don't know anything about him. What they're saying in the news is bullshit. He's not like that at all. It was the reason I stayed to help him out—so that he didn't look like the bad guy."

Not that it had worked. I sighed. I'd known all along there wouldn't be a happy ending, but I guess it's every girl's dream to ride into the sunset with Prince Charming.

"You're planning on raising the baby alone?" Mom asked.

I nodded. "Yeah. A lot of people do it that way these days, and it's not like I can't take care of myself and a baby. I have more than enough money in savings to carry me through."

I'd been single most of my life, and I'd put away any extra cash I didn't need for a rainy day. Now that I was going to have a baby—and had to raise the baby all alone—it was pouring.

"Do you want me to tell the others?" Mom asked, referring to my siblings. "Or do they know?"

"They don't, yet," I said. "I didn't know how to deal with all of that. They're all so happily married, doing it the traditional way. I thought I would walk that road, too. It's what I would have wanted." I covered my face with my hands, a sudden surge of emotions threatening to overcome me. I'd worked so hard to keep it together, to not collapse into an emotional puddle of sadness and heartache after losing Gavin. I was damned if I was going to allow my cover to slip now.

"I think I'm going to use my passport and go to Europe."

Mom looked shocked. "What?"

"You were the one who suggested it," I pointed out.

"I didn't know you were pregnant, then," Mom argued.

That was true.

"I just want something new, something *different*, you know? I feel like I've been stuck in this same pattern my whole life. Work, sleep, save money, work some more. It's all I ever do. Nothing exciting happens in my life. If I go to Europe, I can start over and do it all differently."

"You can do it all differently *here*."

I shook my head. "I know. I just don't see how anything is going to give. My boss has a contact in Europe, some kind of sister business. If I work there, he won't lose me, and I'll have a stable job. I'll raise the baby, maybe even get an au pair or something, and it will be good."

Mom shook her head. "Leaving your support network behind is a bad idea, Paige. Especially when you're about to have a baby. Going to Europe isn't the answer. What are you running from?"

"Nothing," I said, but that wasn't entirely true, was it? I was trying to run away from heartache, from the idea that I might have had a happy ending, but that had failed. I knew I couldn't run away from it, but what difference would it make if I stayed?

"Just think about it, sweetheart," Mom said. "Take the time to wrap your head around the idea that you're going to be a mother."

"I've already done that," I said. "I've known for a lot longer than you."

Mom looked emotional. "Just when I think we're expanding the family again, I have to lose you and the baby."

"Mom, it's not such a big deal," I said, but that wasn't true, either. Video calls and voice calls weren't the same as seeing everyone face-to-face. I knew that from experience after Ava had moved away. At least, in a different country, I wouldn't see Gavin's face on television everywhere I went and hear from Tara all kinds of lies about who he was and how noble she was for wanting to be with him, anyway.

My chest suddenly felt tight, like a vice was clamped around my heart and squeezing with all it's might. Thinking about Gavin hurt like a bitch every time. Would I eventually learn to breathe easy again without him? It had been more than a week since I'd seen him, and the pain hadn't eased at all.

"I have to go," I finally said and got up.

"Don't you want to stay longer? You can stay the night, even." My mom and dad always had room for the kids, even though we were all grown up and out of the house now. It was the best thing in the world to have a sleepover back in my childhood home. I'd always loved doing that.

The problem was that if I stayed tonight, I would want to stay forever, and I couldn't do that. I had to deal with this at some point. I could ignore Gavin and run away from heartache, but this baby was coming no matter what, and I would embrace at least this part of my life.

Even if everything else had faded away.

"I have a doctor's appointment," I said, shaking my head. "I haven't been to one yet, and I think I need to start proactively preparing for this baby. After that, I think I just want to be home to process whatever I'll learn today."

"Sweetheart," Mom said and got up to hug me. "A lot of things don't always work out the way we plan. It hurts sometimes, but it's okay. You're strong, and you'll get through this. You're going to be just fine."

I smiled, and Mom rubbed my back while she held onto me. When she finally let go, I left the house. My family had always been everything. My mom was great about me having a baby—I'd known she would be.

That didn't mean that it wasn't scary. I would miss my family if I went overseas. I just didn't know how else to do this. I couldn't have a baby and stay stuck in this rut forever. My life had always been so predictable, so boring. After everything I'd been through with Gavin, I'd realized that no one else would change that fact for me.

If I wanted my life to be different, I had to do it myself.

That was what I was going to do.

I got in my car and drove to the doctor's office. The ob-gyn I'd found was highly recommended, and my health care covered her costs. I had no idea what health care would be like in Europe—I'd have to find out.

I waited on a comfortable leather couch. There were no uncomfortable plastic chairs in this waiting room; it catered for pregnant ladies, and comfortable seats were the way to go.

I picked up a child-parent magazine and flipped through it. I read the headlines. The magazine was all about childbirth, introducing a baby to solids, how to get a baby to sleep through, and birthing classes. My chest tightened as I flipped through.

This was becoming too real.

"Miss Victor?" a woman in a pink shirt and matching pants called from the hallway. She was young, her hair in a messy bun and large glasses slid down her nose.

I stood. She smiled at me before leading me into the doctor's office. When she sat down behind the desk, I realized this pink teenage-looking girl was actually the doctor.

"I'm Dr. Elizabeth Faulkner, but you can call me Beth." She smiled brightly at me. "Hit me, what do we have?"

I swallowed and gave her a summary of what was going on in my life. I was pregnant. The father wasn't in the picture. I was going to raise the baby on my own.

Beth listened carefully, not interrupting me unless it was to ask a couple of questions.

Finally, she scribbled down a few things.

"You're going to have to start taking prenatal supplements. It sounds like you've been making a point to eat right and do what's best for the baby, but we're going to face this thing head-on, you and I. Let's get you checked out to see what we're working with. You're almost at sixteen weeks, so if you're lucky, we might even find out the gender today."

I blinked at her. Putting it into so many words was surreal. I knew it had been about two months before I'd talked to Gavin, and I'd been with him for about two months, but sixteen weeks pregnant sounded bigger than that.

I followed Beth to an examination room. I peeled down my pants, and she squirted ultrasound gel on my stomach. I expected to be shocked by the cold gel but it was heated.

"Everyone loves the gel warmer," Beth said with a grin. "Let's see what we have." She pressed a wand against my growing belly. Now that I lay on my back, my belly protruded, and I looked a lot more pregnant than I had up until this point. It was as if the baby knew it wasn't necessary to pretend I wasn't pregnant anymore, and it could show all it wanted to.

"Okay, here we go, Mama," Beth said and turned the screen to me. "Here's your baby."

I looked at the screen and saw a grayscale side profile of a baby. Two tiny arms and legs and an oversized head. The baby moved on the screen.

Beth pressed a few buttons, and the drumming sound of a tiny heart filled the room.

"Strong," Beth said with a smile.

My eyes filled with tears. That little bean on the screen was my baby. The sound of the heartbeat tugged at my gut. I'd never questioned keeping this baby—I'd planned to raise it from the moment I'd known I was pregnant—but if I'd ever had any doubts, they were all wiped away now. That was my baby, and I would look after him or her, no matter what.

"Do you want to know the gender?" Beth asked. "We've got a clear view."

I nodded and swallowed hard, trying to bite back my tears.

"It's a girl," Beth said with a big smile. "A beautiful, healthy little girl. She's strong and her measurements are right for how far along you are. Everything looks great."

I pressed my hand against my mouth, and tears rolled over my cheeks despite my efforts not to cry.

A little girl.

"I'll give you a minute," Beth said and offered me a hand towel to clean myself up before she left the examination room to wait for me in her office. I cleaned up the gel and pulled up my pants. They suddenly felt too tight. It was time to go maternity shopping.

I put my hand on my belly. We were going to have to figure this out, but we had each other. We could do it together.

After I got a list of recommended prenatal vitamins from Beth and booked a follow-up appointment, I left the office. I dialed Ava's number in the car.

"I just went for a checkup."

"Oh my God! I'm so glad you went! It's so important and just sets you at ease. I went yesterday."

"Really? You didn't tell me."

"Noah and I put together our announcement. It's going out today! You're the first to know... we're having another boy!"

I laughed. "Congratulations."

"Did you find out the gender?" Ava asked. "Did you want to know?"

"Yeah. It's a girl."

Ava squealed and gushed about our kids being friends. I smiled, but a wave of sadness rolled over me.

If I left to go to Europe, I would still talk to Ava every day, but getting together wasn't going to happen so easily. I wanted to say something at first, but I decided not to. Instead, I listened to her excited babble about how perfect our futures were going to be, and I smiled and nodded and agreed.

Our futures were going to be perfect, but mine wouldn't look like hers at all. She had Noah by her side, the perfect little family. She had all those great friends with kids roughly the same age as hers. She had playdates and moms who could support her, who also understood what it all meant.

I was going to do this all on my own.

It wasn't so bad—I didn't wish for anything else because I didn't believe in hoping for something different from what we got. I was just painfully aware that even though Ava and I were going through this together, our lives were very, very different.

It had always been like that, but it was the first time I wished I could have more.

I shoved the thought away as quickly as I could. What I had was a baby girl on the way, a teammate who would go through this with me. I wasn't going to be alone, and that was what mattered most.

We could do it together, me and my daughter. It would be us against the world.

I'd come this far on my own. I could do this, too.

28

Gavin

"I don't have anything to say to you, Tara." I pushed past her and put my keys in my door.

"Please, Gavin, just let me apologize."

I stilled. "For what?"

"Everything," she said. "I messed up. I know I did."

I looked over my shoulder at her. She wasn't wearing any makeup. I couldn't remember when I'd last seen her without any. It made her look vulnerable and raw.

"Fine. I'll hear you out." I walked into the apartment, leaving the door open behind me, and Tara followed. She closed the door.

I walked to the kitchen and started a cup of coffee. My head spun from the alcohol. It was the only reason I let Tara in at all.

I turned to face her and crossed my arms over my chest. She looked around, looking like she felt out of place.

"You're here to apologize," I reminded her.

She nodded. "I've had a lot of time to think about how things ended between us and how I've acted..."

I stayed quiet when she hesitated. I wasn't going to fill any silences. She had a habit of doing that, making me say things I might not have said because she prompted something and then stayed silent.

"You're going to make me say it, aren't you?" she asked with a sigh. "I was wrong."

"About what?"

"Everything. You, how I acted when we broke up, the things I said on air... all of it was wrong. I see that now. I'm so sorry I hurt you. I just thought if I could get your attention, get you to understand how much it hurt, you would get *me*. You would know where I was coming from."

"You wanted to hurt me because I hurt you?"

Tara nodded. "Yeah. It's hard for me to admit to it, but that's exactly what happened." She took a step closer to me and then another, closing the distance between us.

Carefully, moving as if she didn't want to scare me, she wrapped her arms around my waist. Her body was warm, the warmth seeping into me, and I couldn't push her away.

It was hard to make sense of what I felt while I was drunk. The truth was that Tara, bitch that she was, was familiar. We'd played this game for three years. She was the fucking devil, but she was the devil I *knew*.

"You know what the problem is here?" I asked.

Tara tilted her head up to me. "What?"

"Everything you've said and done can't be undone. The world has this picture of me now that you painted so carefully, and that can't be changed."

"It doesn't matter what the world thinks," Tara said.

"Yeah, it doesn't matter if they don't think you're wrong," I pointed out. "But if they do..."

"Don't you see that I love you?" Tara asked. "Isn't that all that matters? I love you, Gavin. I always have, and I always will."

I hesitated. She put her head against my chest again. "I missed you so much. I missed *this*. I don't care what happened in the past. I just want to move forward with you."

It felt good to be wanted, but a voice screamed at the back of my mind. I was drunk. The warmth was welcome, the company when I felt so incredibly lost and alone, but this wasn't right. Tara wasn't someone who offered her love unconditionally. She always wanted something in return.

"Let's put this nasty business behind us," Tara said. "It will be like nothing ever happened. I'll move back in, and we'll move forward."

There it was.

"You want to move back in."

"Well, yeah." She let go of me and looked up at me. "I mean, if we're going to give this another go, it will all stop. The interviews, the tabloid articles..."

"Are you trying to threaten me? If I don't take you back, you'll keep trying to ruin me?"

"No, that's not what I mean—"

"I don't think we should move in together," I said. I wanted to bait her, to tell her we could try again without being in the same apartment, first, to see what she would say.

Did I want to try again with her? Hell no.

I was trying to prove a point.

"Why not?" Tara asked before I got to say anything else. She fell for it, not caring what the rest of my statement would be. "Why are you so set on keeping me at arm's length? I'm not doing this half-assed. You know that's not what I'm like. It's all or nothing."

"Then it's nothing."

"Gavin, don't do this! I'm trying to work things out, and you're set on being full of shit. God, this is what I mean when I say that I'm in a relationship with two of you." She pressed her fingers against her temples and shook her head.

"My drinking has never been a problem," I said.

Tara glanced up at me. "The rest of the world doesn't know that."

"No, they only know what you told them."

Tara pursed her lips, gearing for a fight, but decided against it. I watched her change her direction.

"I just want us to work. I miss us. I miss you. My life is empty without you. Just let me show you how good we can be. If I'm here and we really try—"

"You're not going to move into my place," I said. "And you're not getting the credit card back, either."

She hesitated for a second before she changed direction again. "Gavin, this isn't about *money*." Of course it was.

"What's it about?"

"It's about who we are together. I can't stand by your side as your woman, an equal, if I have to beg for money or wait for an allowance like I'm a child. The credit card isn't the point, it's how you see me and value me in our relationship. It's what giving me a credit card symbolizes."

I snorted. "Right, it's not about money at all."

The coffee had finished a while ago, and I picked up the cup and took a scalding sip. It only made me feel sick, so I put down the cup again.

"You're missing the point," Tara said.

"No, I think I got the point exactly. We're done. I'm not doing this again. I know who you are, and I know the person everyone else sees isn't the person you are behind closed doors."

Tears ran over her cheeks. She was a master actress switching her emotions on and off as she needed them to manipulate. "You're just saying that because you're drunk. It doesn't have to be over between us. We're meant to be together, Gavin. Whatever souls are made of, yours and mine are the same. You can't tell me you've ever had a connection with someone the way we do."

Something inside me snapped, and it was like I could see clearly despite the alcohol in my system.

"I have."

"What?"

"I've had a connection with someone whose soul was the same as mine. It wasn't you."

"What?" Tara's cheeks were still changed with tears, but she switched to being angry again. She pursed her lips and balled her small hands into fists.

"This is over, Tara."

"You're not in love with her," Tara said. She knew exactly who I was talking about. "You're drunk. You're not thinking straight."

"No," I said. "For the first time, I'm thinking clearly. I'm done with you trying to bleed me dry. It's over, and you can say whatever you want about me on air. I don't give a shit. It won't make me take you back. I don't care what the rest of the world thinks about me—"

"Don't lie to yourself, Gavin," Tara said and laughed bitterly. "That's all you care about."

That was true—I'd cared about it before, but I didn't anymore. The rest of the world didn't know who I really was. They were willing to believe whatever lies they heard, whoever told the story best.

Well, fuck 'em. I didn't need them.

I only needed the people who believed in me, and they didn't care about the lies.

Parker and Ryan.

Noah and Ava, and the rest of the gang.

Paige.

These were the people who mattered. Especially Paige.

"I need you to leave. And I have to go."

"I'm not going anywhere."

"If you don't leave, I'll have security put you out. I'm listing you as persona non grata at the company and in my building. Don't make me take it a step further."

Tara stared at me, her eyes searching mine. When she realized I was serious—I'd never been more serious about anything in my life—her face sobered, and she closed her mouth.

"This could have been great, Gavin, but you had to ruin it."

"Get out. I have places to go and people to see."

Tara must have realized that fighting was pointless. I wasn't sure exactly where it had happened, but between now and five minutes ago, something in me had broken, and I didn't care about what Tara did anymore. I was free of her and her hold on me.

"You'll regret this, Gavin," Tara said, but her threat was empty and her voice meek. She turned on her heel and marched to the door. A moment later, she was gone.

I walked to the door, too. I was suddenly completely sober. I still had alcohol in my system, but it didn't affect my thinking. I had a few things to take care of. First, I had to face my past.

I took out my phone and dialed my dad's number. He'd tried to call so many times, it was on my missed calls list.

"Can I see you?" I asked when he answered.

"Really?"

"Yeah. We have some shit to clear up, me and you."

"We do."

Dad gave me an address. I called my driver—I wasn't going to take a chance on the road, despite feeling as clear-minded as I did.

When my driver finally stopped, it was in a bad part of town. The houses were all low-budget, and people were hanging around in the streets, eyeing me and my car like they were looking for trouble.

The driver agreed to stay in the car while I was inside. I didn't want to be too long. Not in this neighborhood, and not with that man.

My dad opened the door. He looked like a shell of the man he once was. His skin was leathery, his eyes were bloodshot and watery, and he moved like everything hurt.

"Hi, Dad."

"You look larger than life in reality."

I didn't know what to say, so I said nothing. Dad stepped back and held the door open for me.

His home was modest, with worn carpets and furniture that looked like it had seen better days. A single couch faced an old television, and takeaway cartons littered the coffee table.

It all seemed normal for my dad, but something was wrong. Something was missing...

I realized there wasn't a single can or bottle of beer anywhere. The room was a mess, but I didn't spot any empties lying around, and my dad was sober.

"Are you still drinking?" I asked.

Dad shook his head. "Sober for ten years, two weeks ago."

"Are you being serious?"

Dad nodded. "It was fucking hard clawing my way out of the bottle, let me tell ya."

"Why did you stop?"

"Because I'd lost everything that mattered, and I realized if I didn't do something, I would lose myself, too."

Dad gestured to the couch, and I sat down on the edge. He pushed some cartons to the side on the coffee table and used it as a seat.

"You quit drinking."

Dad nodded again. "Losing your mother was a gut shot. It hurt like a bitch. But losing you... that was what really pushed me over the edge. I nearly drank myself to death for a while there, and then I realized the only way to change something is to get up and fucking change something. So I did."

I shook my head. I'd meant to confront my dad today, to tell him what I really thought of his drinking, to tell him that I wasn't going to let him hold me hostage anymore. For years I'd lived believing in that image of him, only to find out now that all of that... was gone. I'd been holding onto the ghosts of the past when everyone else—including my dad—had chosen to move on.

I scrubbed one hand down my face. "How are you supporting yourself?"

"I got a job at a construction company a couple of years ago. It's shit work, all physical because my brain's turned to mush." He tapped his temple with one finger. "Drinking fucks it all up if you do too much of it. Too much of something is always bad, huh?"

"Right."

"Anyway, I work for honest pay, and I keep this place up, so it's not so bad. I talk to your mother sometimes, and she doesn't hate me, so there's that." Dad looked at me. "I've been hearing your name a lot in the news."

I nodded. "It's been a shitshow, but I think it's finally over."

"Good for you," Dad said. "You deserve to be treated better."

Better than the way you treated me? I didn't say it out loud. We sat in silence for a while.

"I should go."

"Why did you come here?" Dad asked. "After all these years... why now?"

"I wanted to tell you how angry I was. I wanted to tell you that you screwed it all up for me and—"

"I know," Dad said, shaking his head. "I'm sorry."

"No," I said. "I mean, yeah. You had a lot to be sorry for when I was a kid, but you didn't screw it all up for me."

"No?"

"No, it turns out I did that all by myself." I ran a hand through my hair. This was a hell of a day for revelations.

"I forgive you, Dad," I said, dropping my hand and looking straight at him.

Dad's eyes searched mine before his face crumpled, and he covered his eyes with one hand.

I leaned forward and put my hand on his shoulder as he sobbed. He'd fucked up badly when I was a kid, but he'd tried to fix it all this time, and I hadn't wanted to hear it. I hadn't been ready to let go. In the end, that had been on me. I'd carried this heavy burden, not because of what everyone else had done, but because I'd chosen to define myself by it.

I finally understood what Parker had said.

"I'd like to hang out some time," I said when Dad collected himself and wiped his face with his shirt.

"Yeah?"

I nodded. "Sure."

Dad smiled at me, and I hadn't ever seen someone that happy. My dad had done something bigger than I had—he'd defeated his demons.

It had been more than a decade since I'd seen him last, and the truth was, I didn't know who he really was. Not without alcohol.

Maybe it was time to get to know my dad.

"But right now I have to go," I said, turning to leave. "I don't have much time. I have to see about a girl."

"The cute one?" Dad asked.

"No, not the blonde," I said, shaking my head, irritated.

"Oh God, no. Not the one who wants to make you look like a fool. The other one you were with for a while. The one who looks at you like you're her whole world."

My throat tightened. "Yeah, that one."

Dad grinned. "Let me tell you something, Gavin. As soon as you have something as precious as that girl, you don't ever fuck it up, okay?"

"I have to get her back first."

"You're Gavin Austin," Dad said. "I've watched you achieve one success after another. You've got this."

I hoped he was right. I left his house feeling like a weight had lifted from me. Not because I'd fought it out with my dad and told him what a piece of shit he'd been, but because I'd fought with myself and won.

I'd faced my past, and it was okay.

Now, it was time to face my future.

When I called Paige, I kept getting voice mail. When I didn't get through the third time, I dialed Ava's number instead. She answered almost immediately.

"Can you give me Paige's address in Seattle?"

"What?" Ava asked. "Why?"

"She's not answering her phone, and I need to talk to her."

"Gavin... Paige is on her way to Europe."

29

Paige

The airport was chaotic. I'd arrived three hours early to check in and have my luggage checked, and I still felt like there was a crazy rush to get it all ready.

My whole family had come to the airport to say goodbye. All my siblings and their partners and their kids—it had to have been the biggest family farewell in Seattle.

After I'd checked my luggage, the rest of my family had all left until it was only my mom who was left behind.

"I can't leave you yet," Mom said with tears in her eyes. "I can't believe you're doing this."

"I had to do *something*, Mom."

Mom nodded and hugged me. "I get it. I understand you've always wanted to break free and this is your chance. I just can't believe this is happening just before you have a baby."

I nodded. It was a crazy thing to do—I was aware of it. I just needed something to be different. I needed an adventure, I needed to change things up so that the life I lived wasn't so boring and predictable. I was going to have a baby, and the last thing I wanted was to feel like I'd never done anything great. I wanted to have something to show for my existence after it all.

"Let's have a cup of coffee. Or tea," Mom suggested, gesturing toward a coffee shop.

"You know they're going to be crazy expensive."

"Yeah, I know. I'll pay whatever to spend the last minutes I have with my daughter."

That brought a lump to my throat. Mom and I walked to the coffee shop. We sat down in the outside area where I could still watch the flight information as they updated the electronic boards, and we ordered coffee for my mom and decaf for me.

"I'll be glad when I can finally have a cup of regular coffee or a proper drink again."

"You'll find your needs might change after you have the baby. Mine did."

I nodded. "I know everything will be different."

"Are you sure you want to do this, Paige?" Mom asked, her expression serious.

"It's a bit late for me to change my mind now, isn't it?" I asked. "My luggage is already checked in and everything."

"I know, I know," Mom said. "I just want you to be sure this is what you want."

I sighed. "I don't really know *what* I want, Mom. I'm just jumping with my eyes closed and hoping that this time, it will be enough."

Mom shook her head. "There's nothing wrong with feeling stuck and like you don't belong. That just means that whatever is lined up for you hasn't happened yet. You're going so far away. Not only from us—from *me*—but from the father of that baby, too."

I shook my head. "He doesn't want to be a part of it, Mom. I didn't expect him to be, anyway. It wasn't planned, and he has way too much on his plate to deal with this on top of everything. Seriously, it's fine this way."

"Hmm," Mom said.

"What?" I asked.

"You keep talking about plans and what he wants, about how it's fine and it's what you expected... what about your heart?"

The coffee arrived, and I stirred in sugar and cream before taking a sip. Mom drank hers black, and she left the cup on the table, waiting for it to cool.

"Did you hear what I said?" Mom asked when I didn't respond.

"Yeah, you're asking me about my heart."

Mom nodded.

"It's not always that simple. Life isn't a fairy tale where the boy and the girl find each other, fall in love, and end up together. Shit like this happens all the time. The whole world is full of single parents and families of all shapes and sizes that look nothing like the traditional concept the fairy tales try to sell us. That's okay."

"You keep avoiding the question, honey," Mom said. "You should listen to your heart. It will tell you what to do."

"In this case, I think it's better to listen to my head. I want to do this. I want to start over and create a life of excitement for myself. I don't belong where I am now."

"You don't belong in Europe, either."

I groaned. "Mom, it's too late! I can't change what's happening. I'm doing this."

Mom reached across the table and patted my hand.

"I love you, and I will always support you."

"Like you're supporting me right now?" I scoffed.

Mom shook her head. "I just want you to know it's never too late to get what you want. You just have to know what that is."

I sighed. "Thanks, Mom."

We drank our coffee together and talked about other things as if saying goodbye wasn't just around the corner. If we pretended this wouldn't happen, I could act like it wouldn't hurt to leave my mom behind. She'd always been there for me—my whole family had. I was leaving all that behind, but I needed to create something new. I needed to create something from scratch rather than deal with the pain of losing Gavin.

When it was time for me to go, I hugged my mom one last time.

"Call me when you land."

"I'll call as soon as I can."

I turned and took a deep breath, stepping into the queue that would take me toward my terminal. I didn't look back—that would hurt too much, and maybe I would lose the courage to go.

I found my gate and waited for the flight. It was still an hour before I had to board, so I took out my phone. I had no signal.

Strange.

I had to power down my phone and restart it before the signal returned. When it did, my phone alerted me that I had three missed calls. All from Gavin.

What did he want?

I shook my head and turned my phone over. It didn't matter what he wanted. I was on my way out of the country, and he had a whole life he needed to lead back here. We were never meant to be together.

I put my hand on my belly. "It's going to be just fine. You and me, right?" My voice was thick, and my eyes stung with unshed tears.

Damn it! Why did he have to try to call me now? What did he want from me?

Whatever it was... it didn't matter. I was leaving.

I was going to a new country where I could start over, where I would work for a firm and have a baby and where I didn't need a man.

Not that I'd ever *needed* a man. That wasn't the point, though. While I'd been with Gavin, I'd *wanted* him. There was a very big difference. I could stand on my own two feet, but that didn't mean that I hadn't grown very attached to Gavin and if I could choose...

It's never too late to get what you want. You just have to know what that is.

Gavin.

I wanted Gavin.

"What am I doing?" I asked, and I stood. I was leaving the country when what I wanted was here all along.

I shook my head and grabbed my carry-on luggage. Mom was right—it wasn't too late, not until I got on that plane.

I left the terminal and walked to the check-in counter. I had to get my luggage back.

"You want what?" the woman behind the counter asked, confused.

"I want to uncheck my luggage." Was that a word? "I've decided not to go."

"Honey, the plane is leaving in half an hour. The luggage has already been loaded into the plane."

"You can't get it out?"

She shook her head. "How are we supposed to do that?"

"I don't know," I said. "You know what? It's fine." It was just every piece of clothing I owned, aside from the clothes on my back and one outfit in my carry-on luggage. "I'll organize with Heathrow Airport to send it back once it arrives in London."

The woman offered me a dubious look, but I turned away. I had another ticket to buy, another plane to catch.

I hurried through the airport from international flights to domestic flights. At the ticket counter, I bought a ticket for the next flight to LA. It would leave in less than an hour.

Perfect.

I had to go see Gavin. I had to tell him I loved him. I knew he was scared to be a father, but hell, I was scared to be a mother. We could figure this out as long as we were together.

It's never too late to get what you want, as long as you know what that is.

I wanted Gavin.

30

Gavin

"Tell me where she's going," I said to Ava.

"London," Ava said. "Her dad has a European passport."

"A passport?" I asked. "She's moving for good?"

"Yeah," Ava said. "She wants to start over, raise the baby, have an adventure."

I cursed under my breath.

"Gavin, why are you looking for Paige?" Ava asked.

"I love her," I said. "I want to be with her. To raise the baby, be a boyfriend or a husband or whatever, as long as we're together."

"Aww," Ava said and sniffed.

"Are you crying?"

"It's the hormones," she said. "Sorry. You won't catch her in time. You can't get to Seattle in time to stop her. Isn't she answering her phone at all?"

"No, but don't worry, I have an idea."

"Are you sure?"

"I have to go."

I jumped in the car and told the driver to take me to the office. I called Dana on the way.

"I need you to get my visa and passport together, and book me a flight to Heathrow Airport."

"Right now?"

"Yes, the first one you can get."

I had a British visa, thanks to a business deal I'd recently done, and Dana had all my documentation from the last trip. When I arrived at the office, she had everything ready.

"You haven't packed."

"I'll buy what I need."

"Gavin... what are you doing?"

"What I should have done a long time ago. Just cross your fingers it's not too little too late."

Dana crossed her fingers just as I told her, but the confusion on her face told me she had no idea what was going on. That was fine—I knew what I was doing. For the first time in my life, I was jumping with my eyes closed.

Would Paige be at the other end, ready to catch me?

I had no idea.

It was worth the risk. *She* was worth everything.

My driver took me to LAX. When he dropped me off, I told him to go home.

"You don't want me to wait?"

I shook my head. "No, it's not necessary. I'll call you if I need you."

He nodded, and I ran into the airport. By the time I reached the international departures lounge, Dana had booked a ticket for me to Heathrow Airport, London. I was a little late, but I didn't have any luggage to check, so when they called for us to board, I got onto the plane. I sat down in my first-class seat and sat back. I let out a sigh.

"Can I get you something to drink?" the flight attendant asked me with a smile.

I wanted to ask her for whiskey. This was a cause to celebrate, wasn't it?

No, I didn't want to drink. I'd done more than enough of that lately, and it hadn't done me any good.

"A bottle of water, please."

She nodded and offered me a cold bottle of water.

"Have a great flight, sir."

I nodded.

When the seats filled up and we took off, I had a knot in my stomach. I didn't know if Paige would want me. Hell, I didn't even know where to find her. All I knew was that I had to go after her. I had to tell her how I felt. I had never been so clear about anything in my life. I had no idea what a future with her would mean. I didn't know if I had what it took to be a good father.

I'd never been more unsure about what I could do, but I knew that with her at my side, we could figure it out. Together.

That was all I wanted. Us, together.

31

Paige

The cab dropped me off in front of Gavin's building, and I looked up at the high-rise. I took a deep breath and let it out slowly. He would be home by now if he wasn't working late. I didn't think he would be.

I walked into the lobby, and the doorman waved at me. They all knew me by now, and they didn't have to phone up for me to be able to visit Gavin.

The elevator crept upward achingly slowly, and the higher I rose, the more my stomach twisted into a knot of nerves.

What if he didn't want me? What if he told me he was serious that he wanted nothing to do with the baby, he didn't want to be a father? Gavin still had a lot of baggage. I couldn't not tell him how I felt, though.

Maybe he felt the same. What we'd shared when we'd been together—even if it had been just for show—had been real. I'd never felt anything as real as I'd had with Gavin, no matter how hard we'd pretended.

I wanted that for the rest of my life. Not a bland and steady life in Seattle, not even a new, unknown adventure in a new country. All I wanted was to be with the man I loved, raising our baby together.

When the elevator door opened, I stepped into Gavin's foyer. I took a deep breath, walked to his front door, and knocked.

No answer.

I knocked again.

Still, no answer. My heart sank as I knocked, and I felt like crying.

What had I thought was going to happen? Either "yes, I love you too," or "no, go away." Those had been the two scenarios in my mind. I hadn't considered what would happen if he wasn't here.

What was I supposed to do now?

I picked up my phone and dialed his number. It went to voice mail. Damnit!

I shook my head and tried again, only to get the same.

For a moment, I stood in front of the closed door, trying to figure out what to do next. Finally, I called Ava.

"Paige?" Ava asked, shocked. "What's going on?"

"I didn't go. I'm in LA."

"What!"

"Can I come over?"

"Of course," Ava said. "Shit, Paige... come over, we're home."

I nodded and left the building, catching a cab to Ava's house. When she opened the door, her eyes were red. She grabbed me and held onto me tightly.

"Have you been crying?" I asked, hugging my friend.

"Well, yeah," she said. "My best friend was about to leave the country. What are you doing here?"

"I came to see Gavin."

"Oh my God," Ava said as she grabbed my hand and dragged me in.

"Hi," Noah said, appearing in the doorway. Warner clung to his leg, sitting on his foot. "Nice seeing so much of you." Warner giggled from below.

"Yeah," I said with a chuckle. "You too." I glanced down. "You seemed to have grown an appendage."

"You know, I just can't understand why my leg feels so heavy today!" He took an exaggerated step and swung Warner through the air. The little boy squealed and laughed, clinging to his dad's leg for dear life.

"They're adorable," I said with a laugh.

"Can you imagine one on the other leg, too? Noah won't be able to walk normally anywhere." Ava giggled before she turned to me. "Oh my God, Paige, if we could drink, I would get us some wine."

"I could use some."

"I have ice cream," Ava said. "It's the next best thing."

I laughed. "Did you eat this much ice cream when you were pregnant with Warner, too?"

"Are you kidding?" Ava asked. "Ice cream has nothing to do with pregnancy. It's just heaven in a bowl. Frozen." She frowned. "Or whatever. Do you want some?"

I nodded, and Ava scooped ice cream for us into bowls. She prepared four bowls so Warner and Noah could have some too. While she scooped, I talked.

"I had all the courage in the world to go see Gavin, but now that he didn't answer his door, I'm not sure if I can put myself out there again. What if he doesn't want me?"

"He wants you," Ava said immediately.

"What?"

"He told me," Ava said and licked the spoon. "Right after I told him you were going to London."

"You told him that?"

Ava gave me a pointed look. "You missed the part where I told you he said he wants you. He said he loves you, in fact."

I stared at my friend. "Oh my God. I have to find him. He's not answering his phone."

"That's because I think he's on his way to London," Ava said nonchalantly, licking her spoon again.

"What!" I cried out.

Ava nodded. "Yeah, talk about a love story, huh?"

I shook my head. "That can't be." I took my phone and dialed Gavin again, but I just got his voice mail. *Again.* "His phone's off."

"Because he's in the air, halfway around the globe, to go after the woman he loves!" Ava cried out. She handed me a bowl of ice cream. "We're going to eat this, watch *Fire Pals* with Warner, and wait until he lands. Then you'll call him and tell him you love him too, and you'll meet somewhere in the middle." Ava paused and thought about it. "Well, not in the middle—there's nothing but ocean in the middle." She giggled. "You know what I mean."

I burst out laughing. I knew what Ava meant. The whole thing was just so bizarre.

We did exactly what Ava had suggested, but it was hard to concentrate on the show—to concentrate on *anything*. My mind kept drifting to Gavin. Was he really on his way to London to get me back? What if he was just out drinking with his friends, drowning his sorrows so that he didn't have to face reality? What if he was just around the corner and he'd lost his phone, or it had gotten stolen, or he'd left it in the office?

Time dragged on. Noah put Warner to bed and helped Ava clean up the kitchen after supper. He went to bed early for a meeting in the morning. I couldn't sleep, so I stayed up, watching *Desperate Housewives* reruns.

Ava stayed up with me. She was the best of friends. I didn't know what I would have done without her.

All of this was crazy. Maybe I was crazy thinking that it would work out okay. I didn't even know. I had to phone the airport at some point and get my luggage back. I had to phone them and get Gavin back. I smiled at the idea of claiming him like lost luggage. *It's a gray suitcase with a blue heart on it, and a bag with black writing. Oh, and the handsome guy looking lost, that's mine, too. Will you send them back on the next flight?*

Ava reached over to where I sat on the couch and squeezed my hand. "You're overthinking."

"I'm not."

She raised her eyebrows at me. "Just give him some time. A couple of hours, maybe. I don't know what time he flew—" Ava's phone rang, and she grabbed it.

"It's Gavin." She put it on speakerphone.

"Sorry to bug you again," Gavin said. "I don't know where to start looking. I'm here, but I don't have a contact number or an address or anything. Has she called you? Do you know—"

"Gavin," I said, taking the phone from Ava. "It's Paige."

"Paige?" Gavin asked, confused. "Thank God. Where are you? Where... you're with Ava?"

"Yeah."

"Fuck, Paige, I thought you left. I'm in London. I... have no idea what's going on."

I giggled. The whole thing was so bizarre, so funny.

"I stayed. I decided last minute I couldn't do it, so I came to LA instead to see you. I had to talk to you."

"I came to London to see you! I had to talk to you, too."

"I love you. I want to be with you. I know it's complicated, and we have a lot to figure out—"

"I love you, too," Gavin blurted out.

My heart swelled, and next to me, Ava started crying.

"Sorry," she mouthed, wiping her face as tears rolled over her cheeks. "Stupid pregnancy hormones."

My eyes welled up with tears, too.

"Come home, Gavin. I'll wait right here for you."

"I'm on my way. Just need to find a new flight."

"Could I ask you a favor?"

"Anything."

I smiled at the idea. Gavin would give me the world, but I didn't want the world. At least, not right away.

"Could you bring my luggage back for me?"

Gavin chuckled. "Yeah, give me your info, and I'll see what I can do."

After I gave him my details, and Gavin promised he would try to arrange for my luggage to come back with him, we ended the call with a promise of seeing each other soon.

"This is *so* romantic." Ava sniffled.

I looked at my friend, and she hugged me, squeezing tightly.

"I can't believe he went all the way to London to find me."

"I can't believe you stayed for him. You two belong together. I knew it from the start."

I smiled. "This story might have a happy ending, after all." I put my hand on my belly. "Who knows, maybe we'll have all those playdates, too."

"Oh my God, that's right! If you and Gavin are together, that means you'll have to move here, and I'll have my best friend just around the corner! We can go to our birthing classes together and be crabby together and have our babies together and everything!"

I laughed. "Let's just take things one step at a time. As soon as Gavin gets back, we'll know what's going on."

"I don't have to wait for him to get back," Ava said and yawned. "I *know* you're going to live happily ever after."

She stood, and I followed her, walking to the guest bedroom that I'd come to see as *my* room. Ava walked on to the main bedroom, where her husband was already sound asleep.

I lay in bed with a smile. I hadn't ever thought I would have the same fairy tale ending as Ava had had, but maybe, just maybe, I could ride into the sunset with my Prince Charming too.

And this time, there would be no pretending.

32

Gavin

My driver took me to Ava's place straight from the airport. In the back, I had Paige's luggage. It had taken everything to find it for her and fight them so I could bring it back, but I had it with me.

I'd wanted to make sure she had no reason to want to go overseas again. She had everything she wanted right here.

If she didn't, I would make sure to find whatever it was she needed and get it to her. I wanted to make her happy. I wanted to make her comfortable.

Most importantly, I wanted to make her mine.

I hadn't slept properly in the past twenty-eight hours. I was exhausted. I'd managed to get some sleep on the plane, but it hadn't been a lot.

Fuck if I was going home to sleep now. I had to speak to Paige first. I wouldn't have been able to sleep until we'd taken care of the whole thing, anyway.

I needed her to know how I felt.

When my driver parked in front of the house after someone had opened the gate for me, the front door opened. Paige stood before me, wearing leggings and a loose top.

She was pregnant with my baby. So much of how she'd acted and what had happened while we'd been together made so much sense now.

"Hi," she said to me, looking shy.

"Paige," I said and took three long strides to get to her before I took her in my arms. When I held onto her, she melted against me.

"You're back," she said.

"You never left," I countered.

"I couldn't," she answered. "I just realized it wouldn't matter where I went, it wouldn't be enough. The only place I can be happy is here. With you." She worried her bottom lip, her brows drawing together. Was she afraid it was too much to say to me?

"I can't be happy without you, either, I have something for you."

I walked around the back of the car and opened the trunk.

Paige laughed when she saw her luggage. "It's a hell of a trip to make just to get these back."

"You have no idea," I said with a chuckle. "They didn't take kindly to me threatening to show them my biceps, either."

Paige laughed. God, I loved the sound of her laughter. I could listen to her voice all day, every day, for the rest of my life.

"I had to find you to talk to you."

"Do you want to come in?" Paige asked. "Ava and Noah are still sleeping, but we can be in the living room. It should be fine."

I nodded and followed Paige into the house while my driver unloaded her luggage. We went to the formal living room, the room furthest from the master bedroom so we wouldn't wake Noah and Ava. I wanted to be alone for this.

"I meant what I said to you over the phone," I said when we sat on the couch together. "I love you."

Paige blushed, her cheeks turning a bright red.

"I love you, too."

"When you told me you were pregnant, it was out of left field, and I didn't know what to do with that information. I had a lot going on, and I've done a lot of soul-searching since then—"

"You don't have to be involved with the baby."

I frowned. "How am I supposed to love you and not be involved? No, that's what I'm trying to say. I want to be involved. I want to be there with you. I want to be a father, to raise the baby together... we can figure this out." I rubbed the back of my neck, suddenly nervous. "I mean, I'm terrified, but I want to do this."

Paige's eyes filled with tears. "I want to do this, too."

"Good. What I said to Tara about us being engaged... I shouldn't have done that."

"It's okay. I understand why you did it."

I shook my head. "That's no excuse, but I need you to know... I didn't tell her it's not true."

Paige frowned. "What?"

"I saw her again after that, but I didn't tell her it isn't true, and I'm not going to."

Paige's face changed. "I thought we were past that. Gavin, I can't keep playing this game. I can't—"

"Let me finish. I didn't tell her it's not true..." I reached into my pocket. "Because I wanted it to be true." I opened the black box with the ring I'd picked up in London while I'd waited for them to find Paige's luggage. "Marry me."

Paige gasped and stared at the ring.

"Gavin..."

"Before you tell me this is too soon," I said quickly, "I know it is. This is crazy fast. But I've never felt about anyone the way I feel about you, and I know I want to give this the shot it deserves. I don't want to just be your baby daddy. I want to be your husband. I want to do this as a family. I haven't had a great example growing up, but I want to be more, and if you'll have me, I want to marry you so we can do this right from the start."

Tears ran over Paige's cheeks.

"Oh God," she said and wiped them away. "I'm so emotional these days."

"Auntie Paige?" Noah's little boy asked from the door. "Ooh, what's that?" he asked and ran to us.

"No, Warner!" Ava called out and hurried into the room. She froze in her tracks when she saw the ring and clapped her hands to her mouth. "Oh my God, Paige. You said yes, right?"

I laughed. "We were getting there."

Warner tried to touch the ring, but I gently pushed his hand back.

"No, sweetie, wait," Ava said and grabbed her son. He started to fight her, but she tickled him until he laughed and collapsed on the floor.

"Carry on," Ava said. "Pretend we're not here."

I shook my head. "This wasn't exactly how I planned it."

"It's perfect," Paige said with a laugh. "This is what I want our lives to be. Crazy chaos and so much love all around us." She grabbed me and kissed me, and I closed my arms around her.

"Yes," she said when she broke the kiss. "I'll marry you. It will be an adventure."

I laughed and took the ring out, sliding it onto her finger.

"It will."

Noah came into the room wearing a suit.

"Oh, Gavin. Hi," he said, seeing me. He frowned when he looked at Paige, who laughed through her tears, and Ava, who had wrestled Warner down, and shook his head.

"I'm going to be late. Are you guys okay here?"

"More than okay," I said with a grin. "We'll hold down the fort. Knock 'em dead."

"Thanks," Noah said quizzically before he left the house.

Ava burst out laughing, and Warner broke free. He ran to Paige, who scooped him onto her lap and dropped a kiss in his hair.

"I think we should make breakfast," Ava said. "Who's in?"

"I'll help!" Warner cried out and ran to the kitchen.

When Paige stood, I took her hand and kissed her. I slid my tongue into her mouth and cupped her cheeks.

I slid my hand onto Paige's belly. She was still small, but I could feel her bump now.

How had I missed it all before?

"I have news about the baby," Paige said softly.

"Yeah?"

"It's a girl."

My smile widened. "Really?"

She nodded, beaming. "Are you happy?"

"Are you kidding? It's perfect."

I kissed her again, and we walked to the kitchen together. I held onto Paige, and I would never let go.

I couldn't wait to spend the rest of our lives together. I had no idea what to expect, but I knew it would be good.

33

Paige

After we spent the morning having breakfast with Ava and Warner, I saw Gavin's eyes droop. He was exhausted—he'd traveled to London and back in less than two days. He had to be dead on his feet.

"I think we should go."

Ava nodded. "Yeah, you two have some catching up to do." She winked at me. "Call me whenever, okay?" She hugged me.

"I will. Thanks for everything."

"I'm always here."

The driver picked us up and took us to Gavin's apartment. He unlocked the door, and we stumbled to the bedroom together. When his head hit the pillow—he wasn't even undressed further than taking off his pants, yet—he was fast asleep.

I smiled and planted a kiss on his cheek before I walked to the living room to watch TV.

Gavin slept for almost ten hours straight. By the time I walked to the bedroom to go to bed, he blinked open his eyes.

"You're here," he said with a sleepy smile.

I nodded. "I'm not going anywhere."

"I thought the whole thing was a dream."

"It feels like it could have been." I climbed onto the mattress and kissed him.

Gavin pulled me tightly against him and kissed me deeply, his tongue sliding into my mouth. His kisses were lazy, sleepy, and he gyrated against me. As he did, he got harder and harder in his boxers, his erection rubbing up against me.

"Hmm." I moaned into his mouth and slid my hand down his body. Gavin cupped my cheeks, his fingers in my hair, and he tasted me, probing, tongue swirling around mine.

Slowly, my body responded to his advances. My skin was on fire, and I ran my leg up and down his. I ached for Gavin's touch, and heat washed over my body and pooled between my legs. Gavin had a gift—he could get me wet and wanting in no time at all, and tonight was no different.

I gasped into Gavin's mouth and cupped his cock. He groaned. The satin of his boxers slid over his shaft, and I pulled the loose elastic away, pushing my hand into his pants. He sucked his breath through his teeth when I ran my hand up and down his cock, pumping faster and faster.

Our kiss became urgent. Gavin mashed his lips against mine as if he was going to devour me, and, God, that was exactly what I wanted him to do.

Gavin's cock strained against my hand, getting harder and harder as I ran my hand up and down his shaft. He sucked my bottom lip into his mouth and scraped his teeth along it, sending bursts of pleasure through my body.

He rolled away from me, onto his back, and pushed his boxers down. I helped him pull them off. He was hard, impressive in the semi-darkness of the room, and I threw my leg over his, straddling him. Before he could say something, I lowered my head and sucked him into my mouth.

"Fuck, Paige." He groaned and pushed his hands into my hair.

I sucked him into my mouth and bobbed my head up and down, slowly at first, teasing, and then faster and faster. I listened to Gavin's breathing come in ragged gasps and relished in the way his body jerked as his muscles contracted. I loved giving him pleasure.

Before he could come, I stopped. I lifted my head and smiled at him. He took my hand and pulled me closer, planting a kiss on my mouth before he flipped me over. I yelped when he pinned me to the bed. His eyes were dark with lust, his lips parted, breath coming in shallow gasps. My breathing was just as shallow and erratic, and the sexual tension in the room grew thicker as Gavin studied my face. He looked at me like he was committing the sight of me to memory.

Slowly, carefully, he started to undress me. He pulled my top over my head and unclasped my bra. His eyes slid down my body and rested on my breasts for a moment. He planted kisses on them before he moved down and onto my belly.

"You're beautiful," he murmured, and he kissed my belly. "I can't believe we're having a baby."

"We have some time to get used to the idea."

"I like the idea of doing this together," Gavin said, glancing up at me. "There will be times when I'm terrified, but don't ever think I don't want to do this."

I nodded. "We'll figure it out."

"We will," he said and planted more kisses on my belly before he moved up my body again. He kissed me on the mouth, his hand moving to my breast, and he continued to kiss me while he kneaded and massaged my breasts. I moaned as he worshipped me, taking his time to touch and adore every inch.

Gavin worked his way down my neck, kissing, licking, nibbling, until he'd worked his way down my body again. While he kissed me, he peeled my leggings down. I wriggled, scissoring my legs to help him get rid of them, and then I was naked before him.

Gavin pulled off the shirt he still wore, and we were naked together.

He slid his hand between my legs and dipped his fingers into my wetness. When he slid them slowly in and out of me, I moaned and whimpered. I was tight, more sensitive now that I was pregnant, and it felt incredible. Everything about the way he touched me sent bursts of lust through my body.

I gripped the sheets as Gavin, careful to take it slow and gentle, pushed me closer and closer to the edge.

It didn't take long before I tumbled into an orgasm. I cried out, and Gavin moved up my body again. His hand was still between my legs, and he continued his onslaught, but he kissed me, swallowing my cries of pure pleasure as I came; the pleasure was more intense than anything I'd felt before.

When I came down from my orgasm, Gavin smiled at me. He planted kisses on my lips, and I drank in his warmth.

He positioned himself on top of me, careful not to lie on me with his full weight, and my legs fell open for him. When he pushed against my entrance, I held my breath in anticipation.

When he slid into me, I moaned in pleasure. He filled me up, and we fit together like pieces of a puzzle, our picture finally complete.

Gavin paused when he was buried inside me, and I trembled around him. I ran my fingers over his face, tracing his profile. He planted kisses on my lips.

"I love you."

I smiled. "I love you, too."

He moved inside me, and I gasped, the smile fading into an expression of pure pleasure as he rocked his hips, sliding in and out of me. He thrust harder and faster, pushing me closer and closer to the edge of another orgasm, and I held onto his shoulders as if I would float away if I let go.

I was so happy, filled with so much love and affection that I could very well float away if I wasn't anchored to Gavin.

When the second orgasm rolled over me, I cried out, and Gavin grunted, gritting his teeth as he held back, trying not to orgasm, too.

As I came down from my sexual bliss, I was breathing hard.

"Lie down," I commanded.

Gavin did as I asked, and I clambered onto him again. I lowered myself onto his cock, and leaned down to kiss him. I braced myself on his chest, and as I kissed him, I sank onto him. He moaned into my mouth, and his hands slid onto my hips.

I started rocking back and forth, carefully testing how far I could go. I thrust harder and harder, sliding him deeper and deeper into me.

"Fuck, Paige," Gavin bit out.

I rocked my hips back and forth. Gavin felt amazing inside me—thick and hard, and I rocked harder and faster. My clit rubbed against him and I trembled, close to yet another orgasm.

Gavin was right there with me. Judging by his ragged gasps, he was getting close, too. He slid his tongue into my mouth when I leaned down to kiss him, tasting, probing. Everything with Gavin was delicious, erotic, but this time, there was so much more to it. This wasn't about getting off; it wasn't about lust. It wasn't even about two people on the same page having a good time.

This solidified our agreement. We were in this together, and no matter what, we would get through it as long as we had each other.

I bucked my hips faster and faster, pushing myself—and Gavin—closer and closer to the edge. Gavin's cock grew thicker and harder inside me, and a moment later, he pulled me closer with his hands on my hips, pushing into me as deep as he could go. I orgasmed a second later and cried out. I leaned forward, leaning on his chest with both hands, and cried out as the pleasure rocked my body at the same time his cock pulsed and throbbed inside me.

I felt him fill me up. I loved it so much more to have him inside me without a condom—it felt like we were connected, closer than ever. Maybe that had to do with the fact that we'd finally been able to tell each other how we felt. Maybe it was because we were meant to be together, and we'd finally found each other.

When my orgasm finally subsided, I leaned forward against Gavin's shoulder, trying to catch my breath. He wrapped his arms around me and held me tightly.

When I climbed off him, I rolled onto the mattress next to him, and he curled his body around mine like a question mark, his chest against my back. He stroked my hair.

"I want you to stay with me."

"That would be great. I happened to have given up my apartment in Seattle."

Gavin laughed. "That's right, you're not in Seattle anymore."

"No, I have nowhere else to be but here."

"Good," he said and planted kisses on my shoulder.

"I'll have to look for a job. My boss isn't going to be happy I skipped out on the whole sister company thing."

"You can work in my company if you want to."

I looked over my shoulder at him.

"But I have enough of everything. You don't have to work at all if that's your choice too."

"I'm not here for your money."

He grinned at me in the dark. "That's one of the reasons I love you so much. Money isn't an issue, though. We have big things coming. Take your time, find your feet. We'll figure the rest out as we get there."

I nodded. That sounded like a fair way to deal with it. I had a lot to figure out, that was true. At least I wasn't in this alone.

I had Ava and Noah just around the corner, and Ava knew what to expect being pregnant—she'd done all this before.

I also had Gavin, who was in this with me, no matter what.

A good friend on one side and a good man on the other, a baby on the way and a bright future... what more could a girl need?

Epilogue – Paige

Six Months Later

⁓ℓℓ⁓

"Welcome to *Metropolitan Prime*, where you'll find the latest celebrity news—and gossip—as it happens! I'm your host, Kieran Cohen. Tonight, we have a special episode just for those of you who wondered what a happy ending looks like. It's a year after her breakup from the infamous Gavin Austin, and Tara Logan seems to have found a new stride."

The audience erupted as Tara walked out from backstage. Her blonde hair was long now and in a braid over her shoulder. She sat down and smiled at her fans, waving at them.

"Tara, you've come a long way since your breakup with Gavin Austin. The latest rumors are that you've decided to leave the dating world altogether. Is that true?"

Tara nodded. "It's true, Kieran. It took me a long time to realize that love isn't everything. I mean, it's great when you find it, and some people belong together, but I realized that it's not for me to settle down."

"That's a big change from when we talked to you last."

"Absolutely. I think it takes a lot for someone to realize where they should be in life, and I've been forced to do a lot of soul-searching. I nearly lost myself after I lost Gavin, and if there's one thing that's a wake-up call, it's losing who you are as a person. No one is worth that, you know?"

"So, now that you're not looking for love, what are you doing?"

"I've decided to reach out to the world. So many people out there are in need of help, so I want to travel and start making a difference. My fans can help me do that."

"Really? How?" Kieran asked.

"I've started a crowdfunding project. You can help out with as little or as much as you can afford—every little bit counts—and together, we can change what tomorrow looks like for us."

She smiled at the audience, who cheered again.

"I have to ask one last question," Kieran said. "How do you feel about Gavin now?"

"Oh, there are no hard feelings, there," Tara said brightly. "I hear he's happy now, and he deserves that. We all deserve a happy ending, right? Even if they don't always look the same."

"So, you don't wish him any ill will?"

"Not at all. He's happy, and so am I. We're just not happy together, and that's okay."

The camera closed in on Kieran Cohen.

"Not one to bounce back from adversity, this spicy lady has found a new direction. Her crowdfunding details will follow in the break so you can get on board if you want to. Ready for a new path? Follow Tara Logan and her travels. Thank you for watching *Metropolitan Prime*, where we—as always—keep things real!"

"Are you okay?" Gavin asked, snaking his arm around my waist where I stood near the barbecue to keep warm. "You're cold. Here." He put his jacket over my shoulders before I could respond. I smiled at him, and Gavin kissed me over my shoulder.

"You guys are adorable together," Lexi said from where she sat on the patio furniture, nursing a glass of wine.

I laughed. We were really great together, I had to agree.

"So, when's the big day?" Emily asked, joining us from inside with a tray of meat for the men to cook for us. "Now that you're baby bump free, you should start planning!"

Gavin and I had both agreed that we would wait until after the baby was born before we got married. I wanted to be married to him soon. I loved being with him, and so far, every second with him had been nothing but a dream come true.

"Maybe when Abby is a little older," Gavin said. "We don't want to have to worry about her all the time."

"I get it," Ava said, nodding. "The first months are tough. Time goes so fast, though; you'll be there in no time."

I smiled at her, and she winked at me.

We'd almost had our babies at the same time. Abigail had come first, and I'd barely had her when Ava's water had broken. Hunter Forger and Abigail Austin were almost twins in birthday and birth weight, and they were about as attached as twins to each other, too.

"Speaking of being paranoid about the baby," I said. "I'm going to go check on her."

"The monitor is on and working fine," Ava said, glancing at the baby monitor screen. We had one set up where we could watch them on a baby cam, but I shook my head.

"I'll go check, anyway." I kissed Gavin and walked into the house.

Ava had set up the nursery so that whenever I came over with Abby, the babies could be there together. The crib she had for Hunter was big enough, and they seemed to love each other. They lay together all the time.

When I walked in, both babies were asleep. Hunter and Abigail were holding onto each other, and my heart melted.

I pressed my hand to my mouth before I found my phone to snap a quick photo. I had more photos of Abby than anything I'd ever had on my phone before. I didn't want to miss a single minute. She grew so fast—they were both headed to almost three months old.

The door opened, and Gavin came in. He wrapped his arms around me before he peeked into the crib.

"They're adorable," he said with a grin. "They're going to be great friends."

"It's so good that all the kids are together like this," I whispered. "When they're a little older, they can play with the others, too."

"It's how it should be—a big family," Gavin said.

He looked emotional, and I understood why. He'd grown up in a very dysfunctional home. He was an only child, but he'd also had a bad childhood. Friends and playdates hadn't been on the cards for him.

I'd grown up in a family with a lot of siblings and cousins, so I knew what it could mean. Gavin now had the family he'd never had before. Not only with all the kids around and being friends, but with our friends, too—Parker and Emily, Noah and Ava, Bas and Lexi, Chaz and Holly, and Ryan and Sam, who were—by some miracle—still together. Ryan talked a lot about dumping her, but I had a feeling they would end up getting married instead.

I loved that we had people who were in our corner.

And I loved that I knew where I belonged now.

"Come on, let's join the others," Gavin suggested. "They'll be just fine."

I nodded, and we left the nursery to join our friends.

"I can't wait to see her!" Ava cried out when we joined them.

"See who?" I asked.

"Celine is coming to visit in a few weeks! Noah just got the call. She said she's sick of her parents and needs to flee to LA, and she gets to meet Hunter and Abby." Ava beamed with excitement.

Celine was Noah's sister. She'd been difficult at first, but she and Ava got along like a house on fire now. I was excited to spend a bit of time with her.

"Maybe we can get her to settle down for a change," Noah said.

Ava snorted. "Have you *met* your sister? Wild is her middle name. She won't settle down for anything."

Noah chuckled. "Hey, you never know what LA might do to you. Look at how things worked out for Gavin and Paige." He winked at me.

I giggled, and Gavin grinned, interlinking our fingers.

Coming to LA had been the best decision I'd ever made. I might have been crazy to tell Tara I was Gavin's girlfriend and pretend to be by his side, but it had all ended the way it should have, and now, we were happier than I could ever have imagined I would be. If that was what LA did for someone, then by all means, everyone had to come here at least once.

My whole life, I'd had stability, a support network, a good job, and I'd been bored out of my mind. I'd had everything others worked for, and it hadn't been enough. I realized now that it hadn't been *what* I'd had in my life, but *who*.

Now, I had stability, a support network, the opportunity for a good job at Core Innovations… and everything else a woman could ever wish for—a beautiful baby girl, a wonderful fiancé, and a group of friends who understood.

Life with Gavin was exactly what I'd craved all this time.

An adventure.

And our journey had only just begun.

Also By Josie Hart

Bossy Billionaire Brothers (Conrad Brothers)

Faking It – An Enemies to Lovers, Second Chance Romance

Secret Baby for the Boss – A Brother's Best Friend, Surprise Pregnancy Romance

Single Dad Bosshole – An Age Gap, Enemies to Lovers Romance

Grumpy Billionaire Bosses (Crestwood Billionaires)

Stuck with the Grump – An Age Gap, Brother's Best Friend Romance

Grumpy Ex's Secret Baby – An Enemies to Lover,s Second Chance Romance

Surprise Twins for the Boss - An Enemies to Lovers, Surprise Pregnancy Romance

Grumpy Alpha Billionaires (Cavaliers Club)

Accidental Baby for the Billionaire – An Enemies to Lovers, Second Chance Romance

Nanny for the Grumpy Single Dad – An Enemies to Lovers, Billionaire Romance

Baby by my Best Friend's Daddy - An Age Gap, Surprise Pregnancy Romance

Fake Dating my Baby Daddy – A Surprise Pregnancy, Friends to Lovers Romance

About the Author

I'm an indie author who writes steamy romance that begs to be read cover to cover.

Bad boy alphas, grumps with a heart of gold, and high levels of steam are my specialty. Every sizzling book ends with a deliciously satisfying happily ever after.

Each book in the series can be read as a standalone, but the books are interconnected through the characters.

When I'm not writing, you can probably find me sipping wine and binge-watching reality TV, baking up a storm in my tiny kitchen, traveling with my family, or contemplating getting another dog, or cat. Or both.

https://www.amazon.com/author/josiehart

Printed in Great Britain
by Amazon